SMALL ACTS OF MAGIC

27 Short Works of Fiction

by

Martha Patterson

Finishing Line Press
Georgetown, Kentucky

SMALL ACTS OF MAGIC

27 Short Works of Fiction

Publisher: Leah Huete de Maines
Editor: Christen Kincaid
Cover Art: MHJ via iStock
Author Photo: Martha Patterson
Cover Design: Elizabeth Maines McCleavy

Order online: www.finishinglinepress.com
also available on amazon.com

Author inquiries and mail orders:
Finishing Line Press
P. O. Box 1626
Georgetown, Kentucky 40324
U. S. A.

Table of Contents

FOR MY FAMILY, THE BEST FRIENDS I HAVE IN THE WORLD:

A best friend is like a four leaf clover: hard to find and lucky to have.
—Anonymous

A drink precedes a story.
—Irish proverb

A LITTLE LIE

Riva had slept with him in the boarding house. She lived in the room beneath his; they met shortly after he moved in—he was an employee at a factory, she was a piano teacher. The five times they made love it was quick and perfunctory.

She had students who paid small sums for instruction on the upright piano in her single room; sometimes she felt embarrassed that her bed was in the corner and she didn't have more space, but after all her students were only children.

For a week she and Martin had a fling, grinding away at it in his bed, an affair for which she felt ashamed later. And it would be hard avoiding him. Two days after it all ended, she ran into him while running down the stairs to a hair appointment, and he was surly and gruff; she knew he didn't care much for her. But, lying to him and herself, she blurted out rashly when they met, "I love you!" He scoffed and went on his way up the stairs.

She felt foolish for having lied; she'd only wanted a little affection back. She also felt a little afraid of his irritability.

One day she found an earring she'd lost on the communal living room table downstairs, where residents of the building sometimes gathered for coffee and to watch TV. She wondered where she'd lost it, but when Martin came in from work he asked if she'd found the earring.

"It must have fallen off when we were in bed last month. I found it when I laundered my sheets," he said, annoyed. "I put it on the table here for you to find. I was trying to be discreet."

Another night, after their fling was over, they played Scrabble with the other tenants in the living room. When it was Martin's turn he held out the letters H-O-R.

"How do you spell whore?" he asked, looking at her with scorn. He knew how to spell the word; he was just trying to humiliate her. She got up and left the room.

But his comeuppance came a month later. One afternoon Mrs. Dobbs, the caretaker of the residence, told her Martin had been arrested for breaking-and-entering. He had tried to rob a woman who lived in another boarding house down the street. Riva wondered if he'd been having a fling with her, too.

"He'll no longer be welcome here, that I can tell you," said Mrs. Dobbs with a satisfied smile. "I never liked him anyway, and he was always late on rent. Don't you make nice to him if you see him again, now. He's a bad lot, and he'll be in prison for a while." With that she nodded and walked back down the stairs to the living room.

Riva was relieved, sorry that she'd told him the small lie about loving him, but she was no longer afraid.

###

SUCH GOOD FRIENDS

Marguerite had been date-raped. This was one of the first things Anthea learned about her when she met her on the front stoop. She'd noticed Marguerite exiting her apartment in the mornings, and discovered that she worked as a clerk in a clothing store. Marguerite was only 23.

Anthea was 54. She'd had a dull job for four years in publishing at a large outfit near the apartment building.

"How did it happen?" she asked Marguerite.

"I invited him in, after meeting at a bar."

"If I'd known it was happening, I would have come down and banged on your door."

"It wouldn't have made any difference."

Anthea was surprised at how Marguerite shrugged it off.

"But listen!—I've been telling all my friends about this fantastic woman I met," said Marguerite. "I tell them you're older and you understand things and you don't have cats!"

This made Anthea smile. Why should it matter that she didn't have cats?

Then, not long after this conversation, Marguerite attempted suicide at another friend's apartment. It was the after-effect of having been raped. She tried to cut her wrists with a knife but her friend called 911. With the blessing of her parents, Marguerite left to spend three months on a psychiatric ward in New Hampshire to get counseling. Anthea was glad she was getting professional help—the rape depressed Anthea and she had no clue how to make things better for her young friend, and she had her own memories of being assaulted. And what, really, could Anthea say to make things all right?

Sometimes she wanted to hang around with people her own age. But she didn't know any who lived close enough. An old friend had moved to Arizona and never wrote back when Anthea emailed her, and a roommate from college didn't answer Anthea's Christmas cards.

One day a while after that Marguerite called Anthea to say she was back from New Hampshire. She asked if she could come upstairs for coffee on Sunday.

"I'm waitressing at a coffee shop."

"Can you handle the stress?" Anthea asked. "Dealing with food and people...waitressing is hard work! Maybe just being a receptionist somewhere would be better. You're pretty and you could handle phones."

"I love waitressing. Takes my mind off things."

"If you say so."

"The weather's nice," said Marguerite. "Let's sit outside and just hang when I come over," she said. "I want to tell you all about my treatment. The shrinks were good."

"Call me Sunday morning," Anthea said to Marguerite, putting her friend off for the moment. She'd never known how to offer comfort. "I'm a little tied up today."

"Okay. I think I'm going to get a dog. For protection."

"Good. Dogs are loyal. But how are you doing now?" Anthea pursued with the conversation, not wanting to be cold.

"Much better. And I'm moving to my parents' cabin in the woods."

Anthea was puzzled. Why would Marguerite want to be so isolated?

"Are you sure you want to?"

"It'll be a relief after the city."

"Okay, I guess you'd know. It's nice hearing from you. And I'm glad you got a job you like." Anthea hoped that was kind enough. A man she'd worked with had nearly raped her years ago and she'd felt guilty about it, as if she'd asked for it, as if it had been her own fault. Some women do feel that way afterwards, she knew. But it was hard to talk about and she wanted to get off the phone. She felt sorry Marguerite would soon be living some distance away.

"I'll talk to you later."

"Yes—all right."

Marguerite didn't come over that Sunday, after all...she'd had a waitressing shift assigned that day and had to work. Three months later, after moving, she called Anthea to tell her she was pregnant.

"But I don't want to keep in touch with the father," said Marguerite. "He won't ever know my child. I only dated him for a short time. But I'm keeping my baby."

"Is that all right with your folks?"

"Yes. They want a grandchild. And they're not old-fashioned."

"Well," said Anthea, "Things change so quickly."

"Yes," said Marguerite, laughing. "And I always said I didn't want kids!"

"Bring the baby over one day when it's born."

"Won't be for half a year. But it's good to hear your voice," said Marguerite.

They hung up and Anthea wondered if Marguerite was making a big mistake, because it was true, Marguerite had always said she didn't want to be a mother. She seemed to have leaped into it.

The wind blew in through the open window and felt unseasonably hot against Anthea's skin. It was almost October. Had she been kind to her friend? Marguerite had said she liked living in the woods, and that was good. Anthea kicked off her shoes, tired of the random thoughts caroming through her brain. She was thinking about how rapidly Millennials seemed to make decisions, how casual they acted about relationships and momentous choices. Had she been that way once? Probably.

Marguerite phoned, by surprise, eight months later. It was May and she'd been completely out of touch. She'd had her baby.

"It's a girl!" she said, "And I adore her!"

"Truly?" asked Anthea. "Then it's good you went through with it."

"Oh, God, she's my heartbeat, my soul, she's why I get up every morning! I'm still waitressing, though. My mother takes care of the baby while I'm at work. And I will bring the baby over. Just as soon as she's a little older. I miss you. And I want to see you again and show you little Cindy."

"Good. Take care," said Anthea, and carefully hung up the phone. She was surprised at Marguerite's easy adjustment to motherhood, but then, that was a step she herself had never taken. She put the kettle on for tea, and the May breeze blew in through the window, fresh and cool, reminding her of all the springtimes of her youth.

###

THE LOST DOG

Mrs. Mueller took her dog, a mutt, out for a walk every day, sometimes twice a day. With her pink coat, frizzy red hair, and beaten-up black laced shoes, Benjamin Smith thought she looked like a harridan walking her dog. Once she had complained to Benjamin's mother that Benjamin played his radio too loud upstairs in his bedroom and she could hear it from next door. He hated her.

He peered at her from his bedroom window. His parents had gone to Quebec for the week, and had left him to fend for himself. He was sixteen.

Mrs. Mueller looked like an idiot to him, toddling after her speckled black-and-white dog. What a crazy old lady, he thought, so hung up on the one thing that mattered to her—her singular pet!

On the Monday after his parents had left, Benjamin found the dog outside, whining for its owner. It had escaped from the cyclone fence in her backyard next door. It had evidently never done this before, but workmen had made a hole in the fence after repairing a drain and Mrs. Mueller, apparently, had not noticed the hole.

Benjamin picked the dog up—it couldn't have weighed more than eight pounds—and brought it inside and upstairs to his bedroom. He laid down newspapers for the dog to relieve itself on. He opened a can of devilled ham he found in one of the kitchen cabinets and fed the dog and gave it a big bowl of water.

The next morning Mrs. Mueller knocked on the front door. She looked frantic and her voice was querulous.

"Have you seen my dog? He's speckled, black-and-white. A mutt. Disappeared last night from the backyard."

"No."

"But surely you've seen him? His name is Spot."

"No." Benjamin hoped the dog upstairs couldn't hear its owner's voice. "I haven't seen him."

"Sorry to trouble you. If you do see him, give me a ring or a knock on my door. Here's my number."

She handed him a slip of paper with her number written on it. Benjamin noticed she had a bandaged wrist—she had probably sprained it from a fall. She was old; she must be at least 70, Benjamin thought. He closed the front door.

He went upstairs and played with the dog for a while, tickling its stomach and carrying it to his bed. The dog wagged its tail and peed on the floor. Benjamin wiped up the pee.

"There's a good dog. You don't miss her, do you? Stupid old woman."

On Tuesday night he got some tuna fish from a can in the cabinet downstairs, put it in a bowl, brought it up to his bedroom, and watched the dog eat again. The dog then relieved itself in the corner of the room, ignoring the newspapers Benjamin had laid out.

"Bad dog," said Benjamin, scooping up the poop with a paper towel and carrying it to the toilet, then flushing. "Bet you don't miss her."

That night he heard Mrs. Mueller out on the street, calling for her dog.

"Spot! Spot! I know you can't have gone far."

Benjamin chuckled to himself. It was his dog now. But the dog had heard its owner and was mewling at the open window. Benjamin closed the window, slapped the dog on its nose, and turned the radio on.

"Shut up," he said to the animal. The dog barked. It was becoming a pain.

Benjamin felt bad for hitting it, for his selfishness. He picked it up, petted it, and snuggled with it in his bed.

"Good dog."

Two more days passed, and Mrs. Mueller wouldn't stop looking for Spot. Outside the window, she wailed for her pet and seemed to be crying. Benjamin almost felt sorry for her.

That night he remembered his parents.

On Thursday, he carried the dog out to the back yard where the hole in the fence still hadn't been repaired, and deposited the dog through the hole onto its own property, next door. Then he pulled a piece of twine from his pocket and tied up the hole in the fence.

When he returned to his house, he used his cell phone to call the number Mrs. Mueller had given him.

"The dog is returned. You'll find him in your backyard. I found him down by the supermarket, in the parking lot."

He hung up without leaving his name.

The next day, out his bedroom window, he saw Mrs. Mueller walking her dog again. He could see the part of the fence where the hole had been, from his window, and it looked as though Mrs. Mueller had seen to it that the fence was repaired. She looked happy with her dog, clumping down the street in her black laced shoes, with Spot on a red leash. At least, she wasn't wailing anymore.

Benjamin thought he had done the right thing. And on Friday his parents would return from Quebec, none the wiser about his little "theft."

###

A CONSPIRACY

Mrs. Dickinson had lived on welfare with her little son for four years. It had been that long since her husband, a car mechanic, died of a brain aneurysm. She struggled with bills and more than once the electricity in their small apartment had been shut off.

One day she took young Jonah, who was six, down to the drug store to buy aspirin. Lately she had been getting a lot of headaches. She could hardly work herself—she had only a high school education, no skills, and didn't even speak Spanish, a talent that could have won her a job as a receptionist at a local dentist's office. They lived in a diverse neighborhood—there were a lot of Latinos as well as African-Americans there, too, so knowing Spanish would have come in handy.

At the drug store, she found the aisle with aspirin and spent a minute picking out the cheapest brand, the smallest bottle. She noticed Jonah hovering around the counter at the front of the store, where Mr. Simpkins, the owner, was manning the cash register.

Finally, she picked the right bottle of aspirin for her needs and went to the front of the store to pay for it. Jonah was standing near the door. She looked at him tenderly, he in his little red Thomas the Tank Engine T-shirt and denim shorts, and the sneakers she wished she had money to replace, for they were worn and had holes in the toes.

She paid for the aspirin, Mr. Simpkins dropped it into a small bag, and Mrs. Dickinson headed to the exit. She stroked Jonah's blonde head as they walked out the door, and on their walk back to the apartment talked to her son about how much they would enjoy Spaghettios for dinner that night.

When they arrived home, she put the kettle on to make a cup of tea, and sat at the kitchen table while Jonah whistled to himself and was preoccupied with taking off his T-shirt. It was hot July weather and Mrs. Dickinson was glad she had a tank top to wear, her only warm-weather top. She swallowed two tablets of the aspirin with a glass of water.

The tea made, she sat down again and watched Jonah as he turned on their little television to see if Sesame Street was on. Suddenly he pulled a Hershey bar out of his pocket and started to unwrap it.

"Where did you get that?" Mrs. Dickinson asked sharply.

"Don't know," Jonah answered, immersed in watching the TV.

"I know where you got it. You took it from the drug store."

"No. I found it."

"That's called stealing, Jonah."

"It's only candy."

"Mr. Simpkins would be ashamed of you."

But Jonah was stubborn.

"He's just an old man."

"I disapprove."

"Would it be okay if he gave it to me?'

"He didn't. You stole it." She was very annoyed.

Jonah looked at her shyly and held the unwrapped candy bar out to her.

"Want half?"

Mrs. Dickinson paused. She knew it was wrong to steal, knew she hadn't given Jonah the dollar to buy the candy, she knew Mr. Simpkins trusted her and would have been appalled that her child had shoplifted from him. But she felt a reluctant compassion for her little boy, and the struggles they'd gone through, and he was so young, she was tired, she had a headache, and she knew it was wrong, but she couldn't help herself when she finally spoke.

"Well—all right. If we share it, maybe it's okay. But don't do it again."

Jonah smiled at her and they sat there together, eating the chocolate in mutual conspiracy.

###

ROBBING PETER TO PAY PAUL

Ariella was an orphan, 18, and lived with her great-uncle in a cottage where she made quilts to sell in his country store. But Uncle Jeremiah complained about shoplifters.

"In the old days, I'd have stolen from someone myself to recoup my losses. They call that 'robbing Peter to pay Paul,'" he told her.

"That's an old quilting term," said Ariella. "When you take a piece of fabric from one part of the quilt to fill in another."

"If only you'd only married," he answered. "Before your parents died in that car accident."

Ariella wondered how their problems could be solved so easily with few suitable young men around, and she'd been so young at the time of the crash.

The next morning she went for a walk. A man, out of breath, approached. "Where is the museum?" he asked as she passed. "I've lost my way."

"Why not take a taxi from the village?" asked Ariella.

"I was robbed!" the man said. "An old man tricked me and took my wallet. One old guy, said his name was McCrory, stopped to ask for a light, and a second old man stopped, too. I'm applying as curator for the Museum."

"It's just five minutes' walk from here." Ariella wondered why he hadn't been more careful.

"Thanks for the directions," he said, turning away. He had a kind face that she'd remember.

"Know how to rob a man?" Uncle Jeremiah asked later, tired, while sitting in his armchair.

"That just happened to a man on the road. But really—you'd never steal!"

"But I have nimble fingers. And I'm worried about income. You don't sell many quilts."

Ariella noticed his hands shaking. The skin on the backs of them was wrinkled like the peel of an orange.

"You know our neighbor, McCrory—he smokes too much. Always asking for a light," Jeremiah continued.

"He's forgetful," Ariella answered. "He must be 80."

"I don't trust people who smoke."

"Our neighbors are kind. And that man who got robbed yesterday—he was attractive."

"A stranger—not worth a second thought," answered her uncle. "Let me show you one of my magic tricks." He balled his loosened necktie up in one hand, shoved it up his sleeve, and a moment later pulled it out from his other sleeve.

"Well, you've shown me card tricks," said Ariella, amused, "but I didn't know you could make a tie vanish and re-appear!"

***

"Money!" scoffed Cousin Jewel, who'd come for supper the next night. "Always a problem. I'd cheat on my own taxes, if I could get away with it! But your father really should have let me be your guardian, Ariella. Because I'm a woman."

Ariella smiled. "My father thought Uncle Jeremiah had better prospects."

"Yes," said Jewel, "not getting by as a low-paid teacher like me. Jeremiah, your hands are shaking! Go see a doctor. ...By the way, did you hear the museum hired a new man?"

"We don't need new people in this village," Jeremiah said.

"New people are fun! I gave that man directions," said Ariella. "He'd had his pocket picked and I felt awful."

Suddenly there was a knock on the door. Ariella answered it, and, to her surprise, there stood the man of whom they'd just been speaking.

"Come in," she said. "I met you on the road, remember? I know you got the job you were after. This is my Great-uncle Jeremiah and my mother's cousin, Jewel."

"I was paying visits," the guest said, entering, "hoping I could discover who robbed me." He sat in the chair Ariella offered. "My name is Thomas Cummings." He stared at Uncle Jeremiah, who looked away.

"Everyone's pretty honest around here," said Cousin Jewel.

"I imagine so," said Mr. Cummings. "But I could swear I've met this man before."

"Forgive my hand held up to my face. I cut myself shaving," said Jeremiah. "Could have been old McCrory who was the thief. A neighbor. Sorry—I'm going to have a nap before dinner." He left the room.

Mr. Cummings stood suddenly.

"He—" said Mr. Cummings, "he's the old man who robbed me!"

"What are you talking about?" said Ariella in shock.

"I'm sure of it! And I made a report to the local police!"

"You're not welcome to stay," said Ariella hotly, "if you make terrible accusations like that. I'll show you the door."

But Cousin Jewel put her arm on Mr. Cummings' sleeve.

"Now, just a minute. Your uncle always boasted of nimble fingers, and this man's new in town, and shouldn't we give him our ears?"

"Cousin Jewel! That's a betrayal of my uncle!"

"As it happens, I believe Mr. Cummings," said Cousin Jewel sharply. "Mr. McCrory's as honest as Jesus Christmas—but Jeremiah's been acting nervous. He likes performing magic tricks. That's how he stole your money, Mr. Cummings. But his store is losing income. Can't you take pity and stay for dinner? The money can't have been much."

"Fifty dollars," huffed Mr. Cummings.

"Then I'll return it myself." Cousin Jewel took bills from her purse and handed them over. "I hope that takes care of it. We'll all have dinner and the matter will be forgotten. If the police come, I'll put them off."

Suddenly Mr. Cummings seemed calm, as if he'd been presented with a nice cup of hot tea.

"Well, never mind," he said.

"We're sorry. And now tell us about your new job," said Cousin Jewel cheerfully.

"Forgive my anger. Working at the museum will turn out well." He smiled at Ariella. "You're pretty as a painting," he said. "And you and your cousin are kind." He laughed good-naturedly and Ariella suddenly felt bashful.

"Ariella makes beautiful quilts," said Jewel encouragingly. "She's talented, and loyal to everyone. And I believe you both have all the optimism of youth. Let's eat."

So Ariella happily led the way to the dining table, imagining good things about to happen in this forgotten little town.

###

THE GARDEN OF REMEMBRANCE

A brother and sister stood in the public garden of a city, looking at an engraved stone marker.

"Michael," said James. "I knew him at school. He was on one of the planes."

"On 9/11?" asked Rachel.

"Just an acquaintance—someone I saw in the dining commons sometimes." Rachel shuddered. James spoke again.

"People suck."

"Not everyone."

A Middle Eastern man wearing a suit and a well-dressed younger woman with a bouquet of daffodils approached. They looked at the marker, then turned to James and Rachel.

"My people did not do this," announced the Middle Eastern man. The young woman he was with reprimanded him.

"Abdul. Be quiet." But her companion persisted.

He sat on a bench. "There is too much judgment in the world. I have lived in this country since graduating from University. I'm sorry about 9/11. But I could have been on one of those planes if I'd come to the U.S. earlier."

Rachel spoke next. "My name's Rachel. This is my brother, James."

"I am Abdul. This is my sister, Afifa. Anyway, I'm sorry about 9/11. Many people in this city look at me as if I'm the enemy. I have brown skin."

Rachel interrupted. "But why did you come here today? To the Garden of Remembrance? You're so dressed up."

Afifa smoothed the fabric of her dress. "We come from our mother's funeral. Cancer. After the service, we wanted to walk for a while. I go to college here."

Abdul butted in. "You're revealing too much about us, Afifa." He turned to James. "I must say, you are both dressed casually for a memorial park. It would be better to wear clothes suiting the occasion. It has to do with Pride."

"That's bullshit," said James.

Startled, Afifa looked quickly at him. "Hm," she said, trying to soothe things. "Let me tell you a fairy tale. From the Saudis. A Bedouin lost his son in a cattle market. The boy was stolen. The father hired someone to shout that one thousand piasters was offered for his child's return. But the man who held the boy was greedy and wanted more money. So he waited. Next day, only five hundred piasters were offered. The kidnapper held out. The third day, only one hundred piasters were offered. The kidnapper hurried to return the boy and collect his small reward."

James cut her off. "The father was cheap."

"But wait," said Afifa. "The kidnapper was curious, and asked the father why the reward had gotten smaller each day. "Well," the father said, "that first day my son refused to eat with his kidnapper. To bring him back with pride, I would have paid one thousand piasters. The second day, when hunger made him forget to behave nobly, he accepted food, and I offered five hundred. But when he begged, his return was worth only one hundred piasters."

James shifted in his seat. "And the moral is?"

Afifa laughed. "Hold out for a thousand piasters even if you're hungry! Pride is important in the Arab world."

"You see?" grinned Abdul. "I wear a suit every day. Pride! For instance, I love my own country for its physical beauty. And I miss the food."

"Then why don't you go back?" asked James, annoyed.

"An impertinent question. I don't love its politics. But I apologize. I was rude first. …May I show you a magic trick?"

Rachel and Afifa giggled as ABDUL pulled a scarf from his pocket, balled it up in his right hand, and waved both hands in the air. He opened his right hand and there was nothing in it. Then he drew the same scarf from within the left sleeve of his jacket.

"You see?" he said. "Nothing is what it seems, nothing is easy. Like 9/11. Like the conflict of living in a foreign country when you are constantly blamed for evil done by others. And perhaps I am not what you thought—I am not "easy," either."

"How did you do that trick?" asked Rachel.

"I read a book by Houdini." Abdul smiled. "And now we'll go."

Afifa suddenly plucked a daffodil from her bouquet and handed it to Rachel. "When you get home, put this flower in water, to remember all those souls who perished on 9/11."

Abdul bowed. "My sister is too romantic. It was interesting meeting you." He and his sister walked away.

"They gave us something," said Rachel. "A fairy tale and magic. See? Not everybody sucks."

###

VALENTINE'S DAY

She was so sick of her job at the museum that she sometimes wished she'd get hit by a car, just so she'd have to spend a few weeks in the hospital and wouldn't need to show up for work for a while. But Muggeridge had just asked her out for lunch.

"It's Valentine's Day," she said to him as they put on their jackets, "And I'll go with you, but I want this to be nice. I'm not asking for flowers, I just want to know it means something. If only the promise of doing it again someday."

Muggeridge quietly assented. She was a bit rude to respond that way to his invitation, but it *was* Valentine's Day. They walked to the bakery. It was only a half-hour break, so they ordered in a hurry. She fingered her string of artificial pearls as they ate sandwiches. Muggeridge was quiet but agreeable. For instance, when she commented that their jobs were boring, he said, "Yes," that he often thought of giving his notice, if only he could find something else to do. Sally was vaguely attracted to him.

She was, like Muggeridge, in her late 20s, and she'd had lovers, different jobs, and had even lived in New York City for a year, but life had gotten tamer since then and now she had no boyfriend. There had been a man she liked at an insurance company—he'd even once proposed they have dinner together. But he was married, and Sally would never go for that. Men! Such a bother sometimes!

Sally and Muggeridge walked out to the street and Sally lit a cigarette.

"Bad for you, smoking," chided Muggeridge. Sally suddenly felt impatient.

"It's relaxing. I'd rather be a smoker than a big, fat person, and food and cigarettes are both addictions," she retorted. She felt unkind saying that about heavy people, but she thought she was just being fair. Muggeridge didn't answer, as he carried a bit of extra weight himself, but he didn't seem offended. He seemed pensive. With his tongue, he toyed with a loose tooth in his mouth and wondered how many decades it would be before he sported a full set of dentures.

Sally finished her cigarette and they walked back to the science museum. She was, despite her impatience, pleased he'd asked her out. He didn't have the habit of contradicting her that some men did.

At their jobs at the museum they greeted visitors and had the dull task of monitoring the galleries, saying, "Don't touch!" and "No photos, please!" Sally had initially thought the job would be easy, but it was hard on her back being on her feet all day.

She and Muggeridge separated and went to their respective posts. Sally had hoped she might have a real "date" with Muggeridge, not just a quick bite for lunch, but he seemed a rather non-sexual person. He had never so much as held her coat for her while she struggled to put it on at the end of the day. But he had promised they'd do lunch again. And Valentine's Day always held the possibility of romance, even with a co-worker who was so timid.

They spent the rest of the afternoon separately tending to the visitors, Muggeridge toying with his loose tooth while he thought about Sally's attractive outspokenness at lunch. She'd said she hadn't gone out with anyone in a while— why not, he wondered?—and she didn't toady to non-smokers. An opinionated woman interested him, partly because he felt he had so few opinions himself.

At five o'clock they told everyone in the galleries that the museum was closing. Couldn't Muggeridge offer her a ride home in a taxi, Sally wondered? Taxis seemed like a luxury and it would have been nice not to have to take the bus home on Valentine's Day. But Muggeridge surprised her with a different offer.

"I was thinking, Sally—" he said as he put on his cap at the lockers where they stashed their belongings during the day. "Like to go to a club tonight?"

Sally's heart fluttered. This she hadn't expected. So maybe they were going on a real date! Muggeridge, she thought, had good manners and was self-effacing, and he had striking green eyes. He had told her once he liked reading the stories of O Henry. She had already decided that she'd like to know him better.

"To what club?" she asked. "The Middle East is just down the street."

"That's exactly the place I was thinking of," Muggeridge answered with a smile. "The Blind Skeletons are playing tonight." He picked up the key she'd accidentally dropped after removing it from her locker, and held her jacket for her.

"This'll be fun," she thought, delighted that he'd held her jacket. She resolved to act a little kinder towards him.

They made their way outside and up the street, where they'd probably have dinner first. Muggeridge took her arm, and Sally felt another little flutter in her chest. So he was romantic! And perhaps he'd liked her for a long time, only she'd never known it—and the kissing and the sweet "good-nights" might come later.

Sally refrained from smoking as they walked down the street. It was her concession to thoughtfulness and being on her best behavior. Muggeridge was silently pleased she chose not to smoke. And he hummed a little tune as he escorted her. His tooth wasn't bothering him right now, and the woman he already thought well of was accompanying him for the evening. Sally was thinking, "Sometimes good things do happen on Valentine's Day."

###

THE PRIVILEGE OF TRAVEL

"You're a published poet?" she asked, very impressed, pulling her skirt over her slim knees, of which she was proud.

"Yes," he said, "by *The Artist's Notebook*, a British literary journal."

"What sort of poems?" She felt awkward asking, knowing little about poetry, but they were having a jolly time over tea, and she had only met him the day before, and after all—he was a published poet!

"'The marled leaves of the autumn tree reminded her of sin—her own and those of her forebears.'" He was quoting something that, clearly, he had written.

"What does 'marled' mean?"

"Dappled. Striped. Something or other like that." He tucked his napkin into his vest and began eating cake the waiter had left.

They had met yesterday on the ship; it was to be a getaway for both; he from London, she from New York. They dined together with other travelers, but this was the first time they'd been alone. It was tea-time; the waiters were bustling about in their white shirts and bow-ties, serving pastries and cake on trays.

"My! I tried to write a short story once, but it had no word in it like 'marled.' And what does 'sin' refer to? An illicit affair, perhaps?"

He laughed.

"No. She was thinking about cheating on a college exam. It was just a memory I had of a woman I knew in school who confided in me about her mistake. At Oxford. But she was rather silly, and I wrote the poem about her."

"I see," said his companion. "But did she regret cheating on the exam?"

"It rattled her conscience. She was young and foolish and thought she'd fail her courses otherwise."

"Goodness! I feel sorry for her."

"She was a fool. And I went on to get married to my lovely bride and had a very happy existence, and forgot about her, until I wrote the poem."

"Interesting."

She sipped her tea thoughtfully, and was very much enjoying this nice man's company. He was about her age, and had already told her he'd been married once, but his wife had died recently, and he was taking this trip to 'freshen up his life.' And he'd been friendly and kind, and so far she liked him. But suddenly their conversation seemed to turn sour, and she thought she'd been as foolish as his former young classmate who had cheated on the exam. She felt like a dunderhead talking to an experienced attorney or professor who had caught her out in a lie, like the woman about whom he'd written the poem. This is how the conversation continued:

"You did seem a bit 'lost' when you approached me in the Double Down room," she said, trying to be solicitous.

"Lost?" he asked, offended. "I approached you because you were obviously alone and I thought you were attractively unoccupied."

"I was watching the dancers and thinking how graceful they were. So trim and slender and—graceful! They seem almost weightless!" She was embarrassed that she had called him 'lost' and was attempting to display some taste in anything artistic.

"Anyone can dance. Anyone can write poetry, or a short story. Maybe you ought to have
tried harder. Or are you insecure?"

"Yes, of course I should have tried harder," she said, apologetically. "I'm not very talented, though. I've kept my figure—I'm slim as a beanstalk—and I'm smart enough, but not at all gifted."

"I wasn't 'lost.' Don't jump to conclusions about people." He gave her a scornful look, a once-over with his eyes, and as he lifted his teacup she quivered with embarrassment.

The waiter came over and refilled their cups from the pot on the table. She was suddenly frantic to recoup this man's goodwill, having made the faux pas of suggesting he'd been 'lost,' and she continued rattling on like a woman desperate for attention.

"Yes, well. I've always enjoyed the privilege of travel—and of being thin. I weigh only 110 pounds," she said with some vanity, stirring sugar into her tea. "And this trip is a good beginning to a summer that seemed a little dubious, when my sister-in-law told me she had cancer."

"I'm sorry for her," said the man.

"Thank you. But her prognosis is good, and she's getting chemotherapy."

"I hope she recovers."

"As do I. My brother is good to her. They've fixed up their house to take tenants in the apartment below them."

"Nice."

"Does writing poetry make you happy?" she asked, wanting to continue the conversation about writing, since he was obviously gifted and she was, equally obviously, not.

"Of course. But getting published was better."

"Hmm. I've no talents. I've tried just about everything—painting, writing, music. No good at anything."

"Only simpletons feel that way." Here he was again, putting her down.

"Well. I love a good poem," she rambled on, trying to be pleasant. "As I love to travel. My trip to England was splendid—so many castles and stone walls and cathedrals! History makes one feel privileged. And I *am* lucky to be thin," she said, casting about for anything complimentary to tell him about herself. "Just last week I had this dress tailored, and the tailor told me I was the most slender older woman he'd ever cut a dress for! I was enormously flattered!" She felt her sylphlike figure was the only thing she had to be proud of.

"Travel is good," he answered, "but is being thin a privilege? Some men appreciate chubby women, you know."

"It is a privilege. One doesn't choose thinness; it chooses one."

"Nonsense. I fancy a woman I can grab a hold of. Like my dear, departed wife," he said imperiously, and tears came to her eyes since she felt she was being rebuked again. She immediately wished she hadn't seemed so proud of her weight—he was obviously annoyed with her.

"My good wife was a hefty woman. Very attractive and not a compulsively picky eater."

"Yes, of course," she said, feeling foolish. "Any woman who carries herself well can be attractive."

"My wife was a prize. And I miss her terribly."

"I'm sure. ...I think I put too much sugar in my tea."

She felt like an idiot. "Tell me," she said after a moment had passed. "Do you come to the Riviera often?"

"Only when I want a good oyster."

"Ah," she said, and sipped her tea through still-forming tears. She was intimidated by him and hadn't been, earlier. She thought she must have insulted his excellent, deceased wife. Abruptly, he spoke again.

"I say," he said. "Care to watch the dance tonight in the club? I don't dance, myself."

"Why, it would be fun!" she said, with renewed hope for their friendship. "I haven't done a waltz in years, and don't expect to now, but it would be wonderful to watch!"

She smiled, thinking everything between them had been set right again. That night they sat in the Double Down Room watching the dancers.

"Have you ever been to New York?" she asked him.

"Never. And never hope to." He scoffed and she was mortified at her renewed attempt at small talk.

"I'm sorry," she said, "for it's quite a lovely place. The taxis, the skyscrapers, the Broadway shows—." She tried to sound cultured.

"We do quite well with the West End in London," he retorted, "and I'm no stranger to taxis."

Oh, no—she'd said the wrong thing again, and again he was irked. Why was he so irritated when they'd had such a pleasant first meeting yesterday? She wondered if she were a moron.

"Yes, of course," she answered meekly. "And those double-decker red buses of yours—they're quite a sight in England!" She was trying her best to flatter him.

"No need to go on about those," he replied. "Everyone does, but it's just how one gets

around. Common sense. You're too enamored with yourself."

Good grief! He was annoyed with her again! He was curt whenever he spoke and once more she felt she was treading on thin ice.

After dancing, which she did with restraint—he danced formally—they walked together on the deck, where they could see the swell of the waves in the ship's wake. The sea in front of them looked large and mysterious. She was nervous.

"My God!" she exclaimed suddenly. "I can just imagine a man throwing me overboard here, with nobody around to witness it!" She felt a little like a gazelle, at the mercy of the hunter.

"Jesus Christ," replied her companion. "Do you really suspect me of such an intention?"

"Just saying—," she answered fearfully. She tugged at her dress that was bunching over her hips. Had she eaten too much at tea, and now she'd gained a pound or two? Her slim figure was her only pride.

They kept up their watch over the swell of the water behind the ship. But her hands were shaking.

"I think I'll go in now," she said after a few more minutes. She was tired of trying to please this man who'd been so nice in the beginning but now was treating her like a wayward child—and maybe she had asked for it, boasting about being thin. For he was portly himself. And she was American, and he was a polite Brit—or had seemed that way, at first. Were her manners so terrible? She made an excuse to him, just to escape. "I'm tired and want to get to bed."

"Do that," he replied, "and while you fall asleep, remember that England is a green and pleasant land. And we don't always pursue thin women. And no one around here is going to throw anyone overboard." And with that, he pulled out a cigar from his pocket and lit it.

He didn't like her anymore, that much was clear. She'd offended him and he was finished with her. What a fool she'd been, thinking he was so polite!

He was rude. She asserted herself; suddenly she felt bold.

"Well, I don't approve of smoking. So, there shall we let matters rest." She drew away from the railing and hurriedly made her way through the doorway into the lounge, and thence to her stateroom below. Exhausted from her efforts to please him, she thought, "Good riddance!" She'd be glad to curl up in bed.

But he felt similarly about her. What a silly woman she'd been, appealing to his vanity about writing poetry and being British!

"Jesus Christ," said the man again, but this time to himself at the railing as he smoked. He could hardly believe that this lady, who'd seemed interesting at first, had turned out to be a typical Yankee drudge, obsessed with her weight.

"Americans!" he said to himself. "Good for nothing! All that chat about castles and stone walls and the taxis in New York. And being thin, for God's sake. I do like a hefty woman, after all." He puffed away as the water swelled behind the ship, and the moon above glowed, and the wind carried the soft moan of acquiescence to fate, and isolation, and—the privilege of travel!

###

A STEADY DRIP

Why hadn't she heard the buzzer? She kept missing deliveries and had to walk to the Post Office to get packages she'd missed when the delivery guy came.

She'd ordered a copy of James Joyce's *The Dubliners* for her friend Sue Ellen's birthday party last night. Sue Ellen had celebrated her 50th birthday. She was the same age as Joan.

Now, a day later, sitting in the hospital with the I.V.—Joan was getting infusions for rheumatoid arthritis she'd recently developed, much to her discomfort and dismay—she blamed herself for being late with a gift.

It started when Nicholas dropped by two evenings ago. They'd had six dates. They'd met online—and he'd spent the night. She liked him; he was gentle and kind, and, unlike her last boyfriend, didn't talk too much.

But they didn't have sex. Instead, they spoke in a friendly way about how their relationship didn't seem to be progressing, and they played Scrabble.

Nicholas won—he had a gift for remembering obscure words, which Joan didn't—she always spelled out the first word that came to her. Her family hadn't played board games competitively, but Nicholas said his family did.

Afterwards, Nicholas curled up next to her in bed, but he made no moves. He had tried to once before, clumsily, and she'd rejected him. Nicholas wasn't offended. He said to her, "Women don't go for me. One of them called me effeminate."

In the morning Joan poured coffee. They talked again about how nothing was "happening" between them.

"I'm not an asshole," Nicholas said.

"I know you're a nice person. But it's not enough."

"Am I really effeminate?" he asked.

"It's not that," she lied.

But she thought that he was indeed too "soft," had a light-sounding voice, and he acted too timid. Even his clothes bugged her—he wore badly-fitting jeans, too short, and the corduroy shirt he wore that night was laced up the front with a suede thong. It looked like something his mother had bought him.

"I'm sorry," she lied again, "I just don't want to be with any man right now."

"Are you mad I beat you at Scrabble?" He smiled. He was too forgiving and accommodating, she thought. Most men would have tried to kiss her anyway, or otherwise convince her they were worth having.

"Of course not."

He finished his breakfast and left.

But this was why she hadn't heard the buzzer—because she and Nicholas were eating breakfast with Enya playing on the CD player, and the music drowned out the delivery guy's ring.

So she'd been late with James Joyce for Sue Ellen's birthday. Her friend had shown disappointment last night when Joan brought no gift, though Joan apologized.

She sighed and gazed at the silent TV in the hospital room while the I.V. in her arm dripped. She squinted at the scrawl of dialogue that flashed at the bottom of the screen and couldn't have been less interested in the soap opera. Her own life seemed like a soap opera. She was late with a birthday gift, her would-be lover would never be attractive enough or good enough in bed, and she had an auto-immune disorder that required regular medical visits.

Could Nicholas be turned into a real boyfriend? Maybe, with sympathy and encouragement. She looked at the tube attached to her arm and wondered at modern medicine. The infusion bag suspended above her head was almost empty and soon she'd be able to leave the hospital and pick up her package at the Post Office.

But right now her life seemed like a steady drip.

###

THE WRONG IMPRESSION

Mrs. Marks held a high opinion of almost everyone. One of her guests at the party was Anne, 22 and timid. They were in a large, empty room, with only a table and a vase of lilacs on it. Guests mingled in the other rooms.

"You don't have to talk much, dear," said Mrs. Marks.

"Then I won't," answered Anne.

At that moment, George, also in his 20s, approached.

"Anne," said Mrs. Marks, "this is George Darling, a military man. George, this is Anne Williston. Just graduated from Smith. And she's applying for jobs as an Assistant Editor here in the city—"

"Publishing!" George interrupted. "My parents forced reading on me. I like self-help books, mostly—"

"I don't read those," responded Anne gently. "They seem trivial."

"They teach you lots about life," George rallied.

Believing these two young people to be hitting it off, Mrs. Marks made her excuses and left the room.

"You look like a peony in that orange dress!" said George. "I'd like to smell you."

"Thank you. I think."

"So—did you have many boyfriends at Smith?"

"We had mixers—parties on the weekends."

"Yes, the guys from Amherst, I suppose. Isn't that school nearby? But that's not what I asked."

"What did you ask?" said Anne.

"If you'd had lots of lovers." George smirked.

"Good grief—how personal!"

"Oh?" He swirled his glass of wine. "Then you're still a virgin?"

"What a rude question!"

George chuckled. The wine had made him a little too merry. Anne felt desperate for Mrs. Marks to reappear.

"I'm getting a headache," Anne lied. "I want to go home. I'm going to find Mrs. Marks."

"You'll be sorry. Can't handle a real man! You could have had a hot one!"

He really was smashed, she thought. Suddenly he grabbed her and kissed her on the mouth, making her spill her wine. She pulled away in disgust.

George plucked a sprig from the vase on the table and handed it to her.

"Apologies. I've offended you and I'm offering a gift of peace."

Anne grabbed the flower and threw it on the floor.

"So much for your gift of peace. You're horrible and uncivilized."

And with that, she left the room. Just then, Mrs. Marks entered from another doorway.

"Oh, George, there you are! Where's Anne run off to?"

"Had a headache and went home. Terribly shy and awkward. I tried to give her a flower and she threw it on the floor."

"That was a little spiteful. Would you like to meet Susan Hall? She's in the next room.

You know, when your parents moved down the street, I thought—little George, what a holy terror!

But you grew up so handsome and polite! The Army must have done something right by you!"

"I make a good impression."

And they went together into the next room, Mrs. Marks to entertain her guests and George to find his next victim.

###

TRASHING IT UP AT CHRISTMAS

An old man lived in the dilapidated house. His wife had died years earlier of cancer. And the Ghost showed up just before Christmas.

I lived in Florida, and the temperature was 70 degrees. Mother Earth had apparently decided that in Florida, Christmas was not a matter of snow and ice, it meant heat. And the weather was warm. I'd just about forgotten my long-ago home in New England, for the river of life takes us to many strange lands, and Florida became one of them for me. I had no idea I was about to meet an apparition.

Appearing from behind a tree, the Ghost beckoned as I strode past.

"You could make money here," he said quaveringly. "There's profit to be made from cast-offs at Christmas."

I quaked a little. Mother Earth was showing me a specter! Until then, I didn't even believe in ghosts. And who the hell would want my cast-offs for Christmas presents? But, as it happened, I'd already considered relieving myself of unworn clothes.

The Ghost vanished, and, still spooked, I suddenly thought of my tatty sweaters and velvet pants that "weren't my color." The Ghost had been warning me against extravagance, with my constant Internet shopping, and maybe he knew something I didn't.

I walked past the house on Thursday, and this time a sign out front said, "Flea Market Christmas Eve." So the Ghost was really onto something.

I showed up at two o'clock the day before Christmas. The weather had gotten a little cooler but was still warm enough that I didn't need a jacket. I went up to the guy running the show. He was a John Waters look-alike—he of the weird 1980s movies about society's rejects. I assumed he was an estate agent. I wondered if he was in league with the Ghost, because he grinned at me grimly, like a stabbing victim on painkillers. He took a quick look at my clothes.

"Where are you from? New England? I can tell by the accent. And these aren't new," he said dismissively about my cast-offs.

"I've hardly worn them."

Reluctantly, he examined my sweaters for perspiration stains. I cringed.

"We take 50% of everything you make," he said. "Tag them yourself." He tossed me some cardboard tags. The river of life—or maybe just the estate agent—was teaching me something about self-sufficiency. And I felt ill-equipped to test my mettle against the estate agent.

To my surprise, the Ghost that had disappeared for a few days abruptly appeared at my side. I felt its encouraging presence as I prepared to decide on prices. But the John Waters lookalike followed me, like a spy.

"You could get those duds at Marshall's," he said scornfully.

I glanced at the Ghost, knowing full well the estate agent couldn't see him, and looked at what other hawkers were selling…old dishes that might have been Royal Doulton, for all I knew, used electronic equipment, and someone was inspecting a garden hose that looked like a dog had chewed it. I scoffed at the estate agent, while the Ghost held up a cautioning finger.

"What do you want from me? It's Christmastime. Don't you have holiday spirit?" I asked the agent.

"I want YOUR BEST," he shouted. "And everyone wants a profit at Christmas!"

"Shove off. I'm keeping my best stuff, thanks. It stays in my closet," I snarled back. But I felt the cold hand of the Ghost touching me on the shoulder.

"You gave up too easily," he said. I heard him sigh in disappointment. Why had I ever let him talk me into this venture?

Disgusted, I left the spot and lurched home under my baggage. I'd discovered that thrift comes at a cost—one is subjected to the ridicule of more high-minded people. And the John Waters lookalike was an evil Scrooge. Mother Earth and the "river of life" were not being providential.

Arriving home, I dumped my junk into two wastebaskets. Who was the Ghost, after all? A phenomenon that magically appeared and then never showed himself to me again! I was flummoxed by my own imagination. The next time I tramped past that forlorn house, I'd ignore any apparitions that told me to be frugal and sell my old, used clothing. He'd probably meant well, but I was done with it. And I did consider moving back to New England, where Yankees are praised for their thrift, not ridiculed for wanting to make a little extra cash.

Merry Christmas, indeed. The river of life was calling me home.

###

A KEEPER

She sat on her patio, watching ants scurrying across the concrete in search of food ormates. It was September, and moths spun around the glass bulb next to her front door. She felt melancholy. She was remembering the first time she had "done it."

Many years ago she had written home to Minneapolis, a love letter to a man she'd known in school. His name was Evan. He'd had dreams of changing society and was studying radical economics. She had loved him since they'd met during her junior year in college, and she'd been too shy to tell him her feelings then. He'd seemed drawn to her, but wanted sex and she'd been an innocent. But she was less so in the letter—she'd asked him if he'd consider coming to visit. She was ready for a relationship. He wrote back that he was spending lots of time with a new woman he'd met, and, sorry to say, couldn't fly out. Maryanne had been extremely disappointed, but decided it was time to forget him. She'd stayed in Boston. It was historic and civilized, and she had a big apartment.

Then she met Alan. He was a waiter, and she was a waitress in the café below the restaurant where he worked. Alan asked her out on her first day. He waited while she loaded a rack of dishes into the dishwashing machine—then he stepped forward and said, "Hi. Are you free to go out?" Maryanne accepted his offer to take her to a play at an outdoor park.

Alan picked her up at her apartment the next night in his sports car. They drove to the theatre near Boylston Street, and Maryanne was annoyed that, on their way into the Boston Common, he walked ten feet ahead of her and didn't wait for her to catch up. Was a first date supposed to be like that? She wondered later if she'd somehow colluded in the disappointment, because she'd made it so easy for him...but, after all, was that a sin?

After the play Alan drove her back to his place. Again, Maryanne was annoyed. He hadn't even asked if she'd like to spend the night, but she was 22 and still a virgin, and she thought, with hesitation, that maybe it was time to lose her virginity. After all, she'd probably never see the man from Minneapolis again. And her friends had all lost their virginity in college.

Alan led her inside, and she asked if she could take a shower.

"What do you want a shower for—?" he asked.

"So I can—"

He interrupted her.

"It's unnecessary."

She hated being interrupted, but she took a hot shower, using his sandalwood soap that smelled so good and made her feel romantic, then came out of the bathroom with a towel wrapped around her. He was already in bed, and he watched her as she climbed under the sheet next to him.

"I've never done it before," she said. He smiled.

"Really? Then lie back and enjoy it."

And with that, he climbed on top of her, mashed one of her breasts momentarily with his
hand, and rammed his thing into her. After a minute, it was over. He pulled out of her and smiled again.

"Are those tears for me?" he said smugly.

"It hurt and—" she said, almost in tears. She'd felt no pleasure, just an awful sense of violation and disappointment.
 He interrupted again.
"It's supposed to be fun."

He rolled over onto his side and fell asleep. She lay awake all night, watching his back as he breathed comfortably in his sleep. She shivered in the bed. She felt excruciating sorrow for having given him her body. In the morning he drove her to work and she waited on happy customers in the café, knowing she was alone in her sadness.

She had not gone out with Alan a second time—he didn't ask her to, and she wouldn't have wished for it anyway. She had quit the waitressing job two weeks later, as it was irritating seeing him around the building every day, grinning at her as if they had a secret together. She was repulsed. She got a new job in an office.

Maryanne remembered all this with distaste while sitting on her patio watching the ants and moths. She didn't believe in random sex and she'd hated being interrupted in conversation. Seven years had passed, and she'd stayed in Boston and had romances that were too casual or turned sour or where the men were cheats. She'd taken a job at a law firm. And just today, she'd been invited to a party by two women at work. She'd already planned what to wear, and although she didn't know these women well, she hoped they'd make introductions at the gathering.

Saturday night arrived. She took a cab to the affair. Guests were milling about, most of them behaving as if they already knew one another. Maryanne, a little nervous, stood with a group listening to someone tell a lame joke, and she laughed too loudly, too foolishly. In reaction, her work friends Ann Marie and Sarah grimaced. She was embarrassed and went off to the table that held a cake, and scooped up crumbs from the platter and shoved them into her mouth. But she wasn't even hungry. Half an hour passed, and she checked her cell phone for the time. Everyone was drinking so much, except that there was one silent man standing soberly in the corner with a glass of wine, looking at the potted plants, and she wondered if he'd talk to her. She walked over to him.

"You look bored," she said.

"I am. I don't know anyone here." He shrugged and she smiled.

"I'm Maryanne. And I hardly know anyone here, either." He toasted her with his glass.

"Cheers to dull evenings," he said wryly.

They chatted for a minute about the Persian cat that was wandering about and examining the potted plants curiously as if it were outdoors on a sunny day. She noticed he didn't interrupt when she told a story about an old pet of hers. The man told her his name was Ben.

"I like cats," he said. "They're quiet and mysterious and don't mind being left alone. Unlike dogs."

They drank their wine slowly and he asked if she'd like to get some air and walk in the garden. While they strolled together, he'd said he'd come to the party because he'd recently arrived in town and the hostess, who knew him from school, had suggested he meet new people. He was a radiologist at a hospital and he told her he liked his job. She didn't like hers—she was a legal secretary—one of her bosses was a bastard, she told him.

"So tell him to cool his heels."

"I would, but he's got a temper and doesn't like being talked back to."

"Too bad. I was thinking today about what would happen if we could all really get into each other's heads!"

"Exactly," said Maryanne. "What keeps our thoughts inside our skulls, if thought is only electricity between neurons? I wonder if mental telepathy exists—"

"Like asking a man if he's bored when you can't wait to leave the party yourself?" He touched her arm with his hand in camaraderie, and she shivered a little.

"It might be scary—a world full of mind readers," he continued. He made an amused grimace and they chatted about the other guests, laughing at a man who, drunk, had put a lampshade on his head and was diverting three women who also seemed to be drunk. Then Ben asked if he could drive her home. Pleased, she assented and said goodnight to the hostess and to Ann Marie and Sarah, wondering if this man could be the sort who followed through on a first attraction with anything special. But she already thought he was nice.

After they'd slipped inside his car, he leaned over and planted a kiss on her mouth.

"I'm not usually this forward, but you smell good and I can tell you're kind and have an intellect," he said reassuringly. "And you don't interrupt when I'm being boring."

She laughed because she didn't like that, either. She had worn L'Air du Temps perfume to the party, and now was glad she had. He drove skillfully and didn't honk at other drivers: she'd hated it when an ex-boyfriend had done that. He asked her about her education and she told him she'd gone to an all-female college and had been a star, academically, but hadn't been able to afford grad school.

"You don't need that," he said. "Piles of debt before you've even finished, and you don't finish paying it off until you're ready to retire, if then! I save my money. I have no debt and I've socked away a good nest egg already." He was calm and he impressed her with his confidence.

When they reached her apartment she invited him in. She was a little nervous about it, but the fact that they both knew the hostess of the party seemed to make it okay. She poured more wine once they were inside, asking him if he'd be okay to drive later, and he accepted the drink.

They talked about music—how college radio was better than standard fare on commercial radio, and how NPR had the best news. He told her he was 35. He was close to his parents and his solitary brother, and said his parents were on a vacation in Jamaica. She told him she'd grown up in an old Victorian house in Minneapolis, where her parents still lived. Again, he didn't cut her off and she felt at least a little interesting.

"I'd love to own a big house myself someday," she said, "to raise a couple of kids in." Then she wondered if the mention of children was too much, since she already knew the marriage word sometimes made men skittish. But he laughed.

"The dreams of a modest capitalist. I'd love the same thing. With a barn out back for a horse."

"Do you ride?" she asked.

"No. I'd just love to have a horse. And chickens and eggs in a roost, and a big swing hanging from an old oak tree for the kids to play on." He toyed with the silver bracelet on her wrist and she shivered again.

"What are you looking for?" she asked. "I invited you in, and so far I like you, but what do you want out of life?"

He chuckled.

"What do I want? Let's see… Books that keep my mind active, a radio so I can listen to the news, my laptop so I can email my parents. They don't live close. I want antiques in my library because they have a past and remind me of history. I want a woman who doesn't mind my runny eggs-over-easy, who doesn't waste money on clothes, who doesn't criticize my cigars. I want to enjoy my job and get married one day to someone who reads and spends Sundays indoors with *The New York Times*."

"Do I fit the bill?" she giggled. "I'm reading Shakespeare's sonnets and I love *The New York Times,* and I only have one closet for my wardrobe. Breakfast is my favorite meal—and I'm not fussy, eggs are good any way you fix them! I'm looking for someone mild-mannered and considerate who knows how to woo me. And I let people finish their sentences." Momentarily, she felt a little embarrassed by this confession, but he kissed her again.

"When you came up to me at the party, I was ready to leave," he said.

"I wasn't having a very good time either."

"Your friends were ignoring you. Are you seeing anyone right now? Are you available to go out, I mean?" he asked.

"No, I'm not seeing anyone. And yes, I'm free. I probably wouldn't have invited you in otherwise."

His mouth twisted into a crooked smile. "Good. Can we go see a play next Friday? A friend offered me tickets to *Pippin.* At one of the local theatres."

"I know it's touring. I like the music. And I'd love to go with you."

"Pippin was the son of Charlemagne."

"I've heard."

"King of France."

"Yes, I know!"

"Imagine being the son of a king!" he said with his crooked smile. "Inheriting land and gold and not taking crap from a boss because you got the dictation wrong."

They kissed and he fumbled with the buttons of her blouse. His shirt smelled pleasantly of cigar smoke and she ran her fingers through his hair. She was sexually stirred but didn't want to go too fast. It was past midnight. They were affectionate for a while and then she said, "Well, it's been really fun, but I'm going to throw you out. And I do want to see *Pippin.*"

He got up graciously, not offended that she was asking him to leave, and after another kiss said goodnight and left. She was stunned she'd met someone thoughtful and smart after so many dates with guys who trailed off after one sentence, expecting her to pick up the slack in the conversation or who cut her off in mid-speech. Closing the door behind him, she felt stimulated and happy.

She began to undress for bed. She didn't mind having laughed so loudly at the party, she didn't care anymore about not connecting with most people; she didn't worry about having brought up the subject of kids while she was with Ben. He had come along at the right time, he wasn't rude, and she was already imagining their next meeting with a full heart.

Falling asleep with a smile, she dreamed of swings hanging from old oak trees, long conversations without interruptions, and eggs-over-easy.

###

ORDINARY

Lisette, in her 50s, was drinking ice water in her kitchen and entertaining a new neighbor. Mr. Johnson and his wife had moved in a month ago from another state, and Lisette felt guilty that she hadn't been the first to pay a call. But she had a broken hand and wore a splint that hung her up a bit. A book lay open on the table.

"Sure you don't want some juice?" she asked her new acquaintance. "It'd be neighborly to offer. It's nice of you to drop in when I'm not doing so great. Did you see me in the yard, all bandaged up?

"Yes. Nothing for me, thanks. I hope your hand heals soon." The neighbor spoke softly with a midwestern accent, and must have been in his 60s. He'd already told her he was married, but his wife hadn't come because she was at a community meeting for anti-gun legislation. And Lisette told him in turn that she'd been married once, to a Revolutionary War re-enactor, but the marriage didn't work out after she'd miscarried. She felt a little odd relating something so personal, but Mr. Johnson was a man who immediately inspired trust. He looked thoughtful and shook his head in sympathy.

"Doesn't matter anymore," Lisette said, covering up a trace of sadness. "Was a long time ago. I got over it. I still think about what could have been, though, with me and my husband. Wonder what he's doing today?"

"Best not to cry over spilt milk," said Mr. Johnson consolingly, "and things always look better in the morning." Even though those were cliches, Lisette appreciated his optimism.

"Thanks. You know, I got a call from my brother," Lisette told him. "He asked if I'd come for supper this weekend. But I've got this broken hand and I don't feel like it. Broke it falling in the tub. Feels like pins and needles when I try to sleep. Like that old song—the Searchers, 1964." She laughed. "Are you on needles and pins about the election? I liked Hillary in 2016, but I didn't like sending troops to Afghanistan. Could have been my own son going there. ... My family mostly was Democrats. But I'm just an ordinary person. Does my vote matter?"

"It does," said Mr. Johnson in his quiet way. He had brought with him an apple pie his wife had made and it sat before him on the table.

"Awfully nice for your wife to send a pie over," she continued. "I'll have a slice for dessert tonight. My brother always says my Mom made the best pies in the world. His own wife can't hold a candle to 'em, not even if Julia Child gave her the recipe. Thing is, when he phoned, my brother asked if I could bring a book over, written by someone in the family. I've got it right here. Want to look?" She leafed through the book on the table with her free hand.

"My great-grandfather fought in the Civil War, on the side of the Confederacy. Like Don, my husband, I guess he wanted action in his life, only with Don it was all fake. But Great-granddad really did it, and he was only 17, and he saw the rough side of things. His family were Yankees and disowned him for it. He kept a diary during the war, and a century later it was published. My father wrote the preface. Dad always took an interest in historical stuff." She paused and rubbed her hand. "This splint sure is uncomfortable. You'd think I could take a shower without fallin' over."

Mr. Johnson shifted in his chair but seemed patient and interested in all she said. She took another sip of water and continued.

"Dad began his preface with the words, 'My grandfather would have called himself a very ordinary man.' He meant his Grand-Dad was humble. But to me, 'ordinary' means boring. Like me. And how boring could my great-grandfather have been? I can no more imagine running away to fight on a side my family opposed, than I can imagine flying in a spaceship." She laughed again. "It wasn't that he believed in slavery—he just wanted self-determination for the States. And a lot of the Civil War was fought over land. He saw his friends shot and got captured himself. He sat in prison wondering if he was going to live to see old age. He wrote about the hills thundering from artillery, shells bursting over his head."

Johnson shivered a little, as Lisette got up to pace. But she felt faint, as if her wn words were transporting her. She put her hand to her forehead and felt dizzy, and then suddenly she seemed to almost lose consciousness. She was spinning wildly with flailing arms, and felt as if she were hurtling through space. In a moment she was in a different world, the past, and Mr. Johnson seemed to have disappeared.

She was at that moment in her former kitchen, years earlier, in her bathrobe, and her then-husband was seated, wearing a Revolutionary War uniform. He was pulling on a pair of stockings. Lisette stood nearby drinking from a mug of coffee. They were having an argument.

"I don't know why I put up with this hobby of yours."

"It's not a hobby. It's a passion," her husband said.

"I wish you had a little more passion for me. I wish you spent time with me like you spend time on your wardrobe. And with Tom."

"There's a hole in these stockings. Couldn't you mend them?"

"Mend them yourself. You're not helpless. I must have had a hole in my head, marrying you."

"And I would have liked flapjacks for breakfast, not some quickly-made oatmeal with hot water poured over it, and no cream or syrup on top. I've got hard work to do today, re-enacting."

"Blah-blah-blah," Lisette scoffed. Don persisted.

"Don't you know the way to a man's heart is through his stomach?"

"You could have made pancakes yourself," she said, annoyed. "Unless wearing that costume makes you unable."

"It's called a uniform, not a costume."

"Well. Can I help you carry your gun to the event today?"

"I'll carry it myself." He got up from his chair with a sigh. "It's not just a gun, either—it's a musket."

"A musket, then. Maybe I can use it to shoot you. Then I'd be a Merry Widow—"

"Thanks a lot. Tom said he'd pick me up at ten. Think he's good-looking? Guy we re-enacted with last month said he was cute."

"Maybe he's good-looking. What difference does it make? What time is the show?"

"The *re-enactment* is at noon."

"Do you want me to go?"

"Only if you'd like."

"I'll stay home and do my work for school instead."

"Tom doesn't like you coming, anyway. He thinks you're bitter."

"About what?"

"Our lost baby. He says all we have to do is try again."

Lisette groaned with contempt. "He's an idiot. It takes a long time to get over a miscarriage. You mourn for the baby that could have been." She sighed. "Anyhow, I have report cards to fill out for my fifth grade class and it will take a couple of hours at least. So I don't want to go today. What good is re-enacting anyway? Just a sport for tourists. And so you can meet pretty young things doing the same thing you are."

"It's fun. And a distraction from what happened with your pregnancy. Doing it celebrates the thirteen colonies getting revenge. It's about history, and revolt, and justice."

"Not this again—" Lisette set her coffee mug down with a clatter.

Don pulled on his vest that was draped over the chair.

"The Continental Congress—"

"I don't want to hear—"

"—appointed General George Washington to take charge of militia units that were besieging British forces in Boston—"

"I've heard enough about George."

"—who were forced to evacuate in March 1776." Don pulled on his boots.

"Are you done?" she interrupted. "It's 200 years later. And I wish you'd stay home and think of the justice of me doing all the housework. You could at least rake leaves. And Don—?"

"What?"

"Do you really think we could try again to have a child?"

"Are you really ready?"

Lisette picked up her mug of coffee and decided to try a different tack. Playfully, she spoke with a Revolutionary accent.

"Alas and alack," she said, flirting with him, "ye do not know me. I, your forgotten mistress, left behind in the barrenness of an empty home, while ye fight the wars to keep us free! Who shall protect me from these battles and strange soldiers from afar who come to wreak rack and ruin on me? What is to become of me? Where shall I lay my head at night?"

Don stood and put his arms around her. She smiled because he smelled clean like soap, and was affectionate for a change.

"My darling," he answered, getting into the spirit of things. "Why, ye shall lay your head upon my breast, and we shall make love under downy sheets of linen, and I shall make ye proud to be mine, my lusty wench! Sure an' you're as stalwart as any man!"

"Ah, me hearty, that's what I wanted to hear! 'Tis like a golden melody in my ears, it is. So we shall have a child?"

But at that moment Tom blasted his car horn outside, and Don had to leave. In a hurry, he put on his coat and ran out without even kissing her goodbye.

Lisette sighed in disappointment and followed him as far as the door.

"Don! You forgot your *musket!*"

And all of a sudden, with those words, she was stunned again, sucked through space, reeling through time, as though she were again 20 years in the future, back to the kitchen where she sat with Mr. Johnson. She was still dizzy and could feel her forehead dripping with sweat. Mr. Johnson seemed not to have noticed any time had passed, but looked concerned and took her hand in his.

"Are you all right? You seem disoriented."

"I'm fine. I just had a little—spell, or something." She wiped perspiration from her forehead. "It must have been opening that book, my great-grandfather's diary, and reading what was inside, about guns and warfare. I'm sorry. I hope I didn't scare you." She wondered what had come over her and how she had been transported through time.

"You didn't scare me, I was just a little worried."

She thought it best not to tell him what had just happened to her and picked up her glass of ice water, trying to appear calm.

"But we were talking about my Great-granddad."

"He was unusual," said Mr. Johnson. "War brings out sad but great things in men. His diary was published. And he probably went through hell. Look at former soldiers who suffer now from battles overseas. Some of them never get over it." He nodded as if for emphasis.

"My ex loved thinking about war and guns and so-called valor," said Lisette, thinking. "Maybe that's why I got fed up with him. I should have been nicer. He lived for the past and never helped out around the house. But I could have been more understanding of his hobby, his need for the romance of battle, even though it was imitation. And we never did have a child. Divorced a year later."

Mr. Johnson hesitated, unsure what to say next.

"Sorry to hear it. But you'll find someone else."

"Maybe," Lisette answered hopefully. "But my great-grandfather was another story. He was the real thing. I guess you might say he voted with his conscience. And that's real strength. What happened in the South mattered to him. He fought on the 'wrong side,' voted, you could say, with body and soul. Afterwards he made up with his family, got married, had kids, and became a judge in Tennessee."

Mr. Johnson smiled and didn't interrupt. Lisette felt proud all of a sudden.

"'Ordinary?' My great-grandfather was a renegade! So when I vote in November, I'll think of him, willing to take a stand. This country was broken in two during the Civil War—like my hand. But when it healed, it was stronger. There's always hope, and you gotta vote." She rubbed her hand again. "This hand bothers me most when I'm trying to fall asleep. I should never have slipped like I did. But maybe I'll keep a diary, too, once I can write again. About how I vote and what I think about this country! Everything a person does matters. And maybe I'm not so ordinary myself, after all." She paused.

"I should tell you. Turned out my husband Don was gay, had an affair with his buddy Tom. And all the while I'm thinking, well, do I have to be jealous of the men, too? 'Cause he never really looked at other women, unless they were also re-enactors. And even then it was just for their costumes—*uniforms*, as Don would have said."

She touched her broken hand.

"What he really liked was men. Anyway, enough about that. Glad you dropped in. A move like yours from another state is hard, and really, I should have been the one to visit you first. Make sure you thank your wife for the pie."

She stopped herself, feeling as if she were ushering him out and expecting him to leave. She felt as though she were in a warp of distance, time, and history. Thinking better of her quickly-uttered words, she spoke again.

"Sure you wouldn't even like a little iced tea? I could make some up real quick."

###

A DILEMMA

Anna was volunteering in the church office and she and Theresa could hear the organist practicing in the sanctuary. Stuffing envelopes for a mailing, Anna got a paper cut. Theresa held a tissue out to her to stanch the blood.

"Thanks," said Anna.

"I'm glad you're here," Theresa answered kindly. "Most volunteers don't stay more than a day. I'll buy you lunch."

"Thank you."

Theresa handed a restaurant flier to Anna.

"Here's the take-out menu. Order a sub sandwich or something."
was grateful and hungry, since it was almost 1:00pm. Tossing the tissue into the trash, she said, "I'll have a tuna sub. With extra mayo."

"Wise up with the mayo. You don't want to be The Fatted Calf, now, do you?"

Anna laughed.

"'The Fatted Calf.' Where does that expression come from?"

"A metaphor," answered Theresa. "Celebrating the long-awaited return of someone. In the New Testament people kept one special animal to fatten it up. Killing it was done on rare occasions. When the prodigal son came back, the father "killed the fatted calf" to demonstrate that the occasion was out of the ordinary."

"Hmm," said Anna. "I'll take my tuna sub without the extra mayo. Okay?" She handed the menu back to Theresa.

"Good choice."

"You know," said Anna, "it makes me feel peaceful to be here, in the office of a church.

Maybe it's the music coming from the organist. Harmonious. Funny how you remember your parents at times like this."

"Your parents have passed?"

"Yes. And you know, I still feel anger towards them. I wish I didn't, but my father was bitter when he got old, and my mother thought I never made enough of myself. I'd like to forgive them."

"Familiar story."

"But this music makes me feel forgiving," continued Anna. "I keep thinking to myself, 'Well, they loved me.' Probably more than anyone else ever has. And they gave me food and shelter and all the normal things parents are supposed to."

Theresa rolled her eyes at the ceiling.

"Tell me about love. My mother has Alzheimer's, my father isn't doing too well. He has sciatica, a heart murmur, bad teeth. They're a handful. I'm flying to North Carolina this weekend to check up on them."

"Good of you. I hope you have a safe trip. Tell me, who reads the requests for prayers in these donor envelopes? The Priest?"

Theresa smiled.

"Our Blessed Mother reads them."

Anna laughed.

"Really?"

"Of course. If the Priest read them he'd have no time for anything else."

"The Blessed Mother must stay busy," Anna replied.

She finished her work and departed, after saying goodbye to Theresa. As she walked down the street she thought she'd stop in at her own church for Confession. The steps at the cathedral were muddy from the recent rain and she regretted not having worn boots that day. Something from her past lingered in her mind, something she never talked to anyone about but that had left her feeling sad. She wanted words of wisdom from the priest.

"…It was horrible," confessed Anna to him. "Horrible of me to do it, and horrible of him as well—"

"Er—yes," said the Priest. "Maybe you could start at the beginning."

"I struggled so—" said Anna, holding back tears.

"Perhaps I've missed something," said the Priest. "—I can't help you if I don't know what happened."

Anna took a deep breath. How could she describe something of which she was so ashamed?

"I went for a walk in the park one day—suddenly I ached—I felt my head had been split in two, by the power of the sun shining down on me—"

"The sun has a marvelous power to soothe the soul," answered the Priest.

"It was excruciating. I really felt as if I were being punished. Don't you get it?" replied Anna. "I was suffering—

"Ah. You were in pain. But you struggled over what?"

"The whole thing—this man I loved. And my own self-doubt. I collapsed on a bench, and I felt as if an axe had been thrown at my skull. Or was it God? I knew I had done wrong. I feel so stupid sometimes."

She remembered that afternoon—the sunshine, the force of the blow that seemed to strike her. How could she describe it to this Priest?

"I'd approached a guy on a bench," she continued, "just wanting friendship, or comfort, or something. I talked to him for a minute but then he asked for money. I had no money, and that wasn't why I was there, anyway. I just wanted to talk to a kindred soul."

"Even I feel unintelligent sometimes! This is what is known as human frailty," the priest answered.

"Is that all it was? My transgression? Just an incidence of frailty? Because I thought it was more than that—I thought I must be evil."

Suddenly the Priest interrupted her.

"Sorry—a button just fell off my shirt. Drat. What was that you said about going for a walk? I don't know exactly what happened."

"A button? Get one of the nuns to sew it back on for you. ...I can't tell you exactly what happened. It's embarrassing. But I made a terrible mistake—"

"Anna, I have heard much before. Everyone makes many mistakes in her life. You must forgive yourself first, and then you will come to forgive others."

Anna blurted out, impatient with the Priest.

"But I felt as if the Devil had taken over me! I thought I saw God, and he blamed me. Because I hadn't respected someone else's marriage."

"Marriage? Then you are talking about sacrilege. We must always respect commitments.

My Child, we only seek our information from God. Tremendous battles are fought against the Devil on behalf of God, and so it is that the Devil is made weak. But you are not the Devil. And no one can see God. He is manifest in us but he is not flesh, since Christ died in His name. You had a crisis in faith, and that crisis is over. You are home now, and you are forgiven."

"I wonder if I'll ever stop feeling guilty," she said.

"Your sin is still something of a mystery to me. But you asked to be redeemed. Pray for redemption and light."

"I do."

"'Time heals all wounds,'" said the Priest. "And you will be healed."

"Thank you." Anna stood and then left the church, carefully trying to step over the mud in front so as not to dirty her shoes. But the priest hadn't really understood her crisis, and she still felt upset. The next day, Anna and Theresa again sat in the church where Anna volunteered. They were sorting donor envelopes.

"Theresa, are you married?"

"I was. He died."

"I'm sorry."

"Brain aneurysm."

"How terrible." Anna watched Theresa, but Theresa seemed calm.

"Things happen."

Anna hesitated before speaking.

"Oh, I know, believe me. Terrible things have happened to ME."

"What sort of things?"

"It's just—well, a married man. And how I betrayed myself. I can't talk about it right now. But I felt as if I'd lost my faith."

Theresa smiled.

"You came to work here for a reason. You can tell me. I've heard it all—from people who
come to our Sunday service, people who stop in to say hello, people on their way home after a funeral."

Anna began to cry.

"It was someone I never should have been with. But he seemed strong, and smart, and he was generous to me and he told me I was beautiful. No one had ever said that to me before. He was separated from his wife. I didn't know they were trying to get back together. He said it was over between them. And I believed it. And I used to feel, with him, that if life could go on like that forever, I'd never need religion or God or anything else in my life—just him. And then, as quickly as it began, it ended."

"What happened?" Theresa asked gently.

"He got fed up with me. He knew the affair bothered my conscience."

"He went back to his wife?"

"They tried to reunite. Then got divorced. I'm so ashamed."

Theresa laid a donor card firmly on the table.

"And this made you question your right to exist—?"

"It did. He said I was indecisive, couldn't commit to anything. It wasn't fear of his wife—she never found out, and ended up leaving him anyway—but I was afraid of myself."

"A bad choice," answered Theresa with some sympathy. "I can understand being tempted, and even getting involved with him, but I can't understand feeling worthless. It probably wasn't your fault. And it wasn't a hit-and-run accident, you didn't molest any children, you never murdered anyone! Don't keep blaming yourself."

"Maybe you would understand better if you'd betrayed your own heart."

Theresa reached out and touched Anna's hand.

"You're still a kid. You'll get over it."

Anna drew her hand away. She was suddenly irritated with Theresa for not understanding.

"Look at you! You've got everything you want. A nice job, a place to work where people like you, family you care for. And I felt as if I'd lost everything—not just him, but my soul, my peace of mind, my character. I didn't understand myself. And after all, what do you have to worry about in life? Everybody likes you and you've got a good job. You're secure."

Theresa shook her head.

"I worry."

"Do you?" asked Anna. "You seem to coast along, content with everything."

Theresa chuckled.

"Coast? I worry about paying my taxes, I worry about my parents' health, I worry about dying, for Heaven's sake! Nothing in life comes easy."

"But you're cheerful anyway. I wish I were. Maybe I have too strong a conscience. I know I'm naïve. And try as I can, I can't find anything to feel good about."

Theresa leaned forward.

"Let me tell you something. You're younger than I am, and I can tell you've had trouble. You may have made bad choices, but they're in the past. It may have been love, it may have been sex, it may have been only a trivial affair. But nothing—NOTHING—can take away God's love."

"It's hard to believe that when everything's upside down. This man—he took my identity. My self-respect."

"You did it yourself."

Anna nodded.

"Yes, but—I didn't know it at the time."

"You do now. You learned something. And you're a better person now. Listen to me. I feel God's love every day."

"Do you?"

Theresa leaned forward and spoke with vehemence.

"I do. I feel it when I look at the tulips I grow in my garden. When I watch a beautiful blue jay on my lawn. I feel it every time I see my young nephew who's leaving soon for college. And I'm not always a good person, Anna. I try, but I don't always manage."

"You never had kids of your own?"

"No. But I've come to terms with that. I'm getting old. But I find light every day. It's everywhere, it's the moon shining through my window when I go to sleep, it's my Starbuck's coffee in the morning, it's even the way the bus that picks me up for work always gets to the stop just when I do, like clockwork! There are plenty of good things in life."

Anna smiled.

"So what you're telling me is, 'Thank God for small favors?' "

"Exactly. I'm grateful for so many things. The way this church welcomes me as part of the congregation. The way all our visitors appreciate the work I do. And I'm thankful for you, because you show up to volunteer, you don't complain, and—you're a friend!"

Anna nodded.

"I do find you comforting," she said. "And the priest at my church—well, his mind wanders and he doesn't always understand what I say at Confession. But you've helped."

"We're two hearts beating in the same room," answered Theresa. She smiled. "It's company. Sometimes I think I'd like to get a cat, just to have another heart beating in my house. I haven't got one. But I have friends, I have relatives, and here—I have you!"

"You're very kind," said Anna. "Thanks. I'm finished—but I'll be back tomorrow."

She put on her jacket.

"You lifted my spirits. Thanks."

Theresa waved her out of the room.

"Bye."

Later, Anna went back to the Priest at her own church. The steps of the cathedral were no longer muddy. The sun shone and she was feeling a bit more at peace.

"…And so I suppose it was Divine Will that brought me to my volunteer job," she told him. "I feel so happy there. I found a place where I belong, where I'm accepted just for who I am. Theresa is so nice. She shares her thoughts with me. And I felt so much anguish before. I'm still young, and she's older. She comforts me. …Father, can I tell you something? It's silly."

"This is Confession—you may tell me anything." The Priest coughed as if he had a cold.

"When I was a little girl, I was a Girl Scout. And we used to go camping in the woods. And we made pancakes on Bunson Burners, and gathered firewood, and I was a Bubble Dancer."

"And what is a 'Bubble Dancer,' my Child?"

"—That meant I was the one who washed dishes."

"I see." The Priest coughed again and phlegm rattled in his throat. He seemed distracted.

"But what does this have to do with your job at the church?" he continued.

"It was fun, that's all. Another nice memory, that makes me feel as if I have a right to be."

"You do, Anna. You are a child of God."

"Father—was I a Lost Lamb?"

Suddenly Anna heard the Priest's shoe scuffling on the floor. He had changed the subject.

"Drat. The sole of my shoe…it's come off."

"What?" replied Anna, startled.

"The sole of my loafer. It's loose."

Anna wished he would stop coughing and clearing his throat.

"Then go to a cobbler," she replied. "Easy enough to have it repaired."

The Priest paused, then spoke.

"I can't manage things anymore…" he said. She felt he was struggling to listen to her, and was annoyed that she had to comfort him instead of the other way around.

"Father, I'm talking to you."

"Yes, yes. I'm sorry. I was distracted for a moment. A cobbler. …What were you saying?"

"I felt like a Lost Lamb."

"Ah, yes," said the Priest, resuming his counsel. "We are all Lost Lambs. But God finds a path for everyone."

Anna sighed. She wished she were back in the office with Theresa instead of listening to this tiresome priest.

"Sometimes it seems like that path is a long time in coming."

"Things take time," said the Priest. "But God hears everyone. He does not bring us good weather on our wedding day, or a promising new job, or whatever else we might request, just because we ask for it. He is not simple. He reconciles us to each other, and he makes us Holy."

"Theresa at my volunteer job made me realize there's so much hope and goodness in the world. And it's strange, but I was sitting in the sunshine at work yesterday, and I felt benevolence pouring down on me through the window."

"That is good," said the Priest.

Anna continued.

"And at that moment, the mistakes I've made in life seemed almost meaningless, as if I could overcome anything. Theresa made me feel that way. She's wise."

"She's a true friend."

"Yes," Anna responded. "Anyway…I think now—I mean, I KNOW—that my conscience is clear. At last. You see, I'd never wanted to come between any man and his wife. I never thought I would. My parents were content together—not the happiest of couples, maybe, but they stayed together. And I respect that. I respect it tremendously."

The Priest cut her off.

"My shoe—I'm sorry, Anna. I get distracted. I've done a lot of walking in these shoes of mine. Time to get a new pair."

"Father? Do you hear me? Your shoes really don't matter too much to me right now. Can't you just listen?" Anna caught herself, feeling abrupt and rude. "—I apologize. Maybe your shoes are important to you."

The Priest coughed again.

"I have a cold. So sorry. I do hear you. People—sometimes quite ordinary people—lead us back to life. We find our own souls reflected in someone else."

"Yes, quite. That's the way it is." Anna bowed her head. "I've returned to faith. Life is better with kindred spirits—good people, the ones who don't put you down but instead hold your hand and lift you up. Theresa does that. And I made the biggest mistake of my life, but she likes me anyway. And she's glad when I come to work with her. Thank goodness for a friend. And thank you, Father. I do hope you get a new pair of shoes!"

She left and tried to forget about the priest with his trivial problems. Maybe hers seemed trivial to him. But Theresa had woken her up to the blessings of faith and forgiveness. She tripped down the front steps feeling lighter and happier than she'd been in months. And tomorrow she'd see Theresa again and maybe they'd have lunch together. The Priest, as wise as he was supposed to be, had actually been of less help than her co-worker. Well, he was old and had been hearing confessions for a long time. He was probably tired and bored with his work. But she'd see Theresa tomorrow and maybe they'd confide in each other again. She felt as if her long-awaited return to the "land of the living" should be celebrated—she remembered Theresa's story about the Fatted Calf offered in sacrifice. She forgave herself, at last, for being involved in infidelity and the betrayal of a marriage, and thought she had new reason to live. And she knew her mistake would never happen again. Today already seemed brighter. The sun was out and she saw a blue jay on the sidewalk, like the one Theresa had mentioned. It pecked at the grass and just watching it made her feel happy. She had found her soul again.

###

HOME

It was a rainy night in September, during Eisenhower's presidency. The fall leaves, just about to turn color, were dripping and Leonard could smell worms crawling on the sidewalk. A roommate of his in college had said once he could always "smell the worms" when it rained. It would be Halloween soon, and children would be collecting candy. Leonard hoped it wouldn't rain that night so the kids wouldn't be stepping on odorous worms.

Leonard Wadsworth, on a lonely mission after dining solo at The Lost Fisherman's Pub, was headed home, about to tell his wife he'd no longer provide her with provender for her over-large stomach and frippery for her ample bosom. He wore high-waisted pants, as it was the 1950s, and he'd always copied jazz musicians in their style of dress. He'd had enough unfaithfulness from Lucy for twelve men, nay, for an army in Korea, he thought regretfully as he remembered his draft-dodging, if only he'd been wise enough to serve in the military instead of marrying such worthless trash as Lucy had proved to be!

Eisenhower had threatened to use nuclear weapons unless China disengaged from involvement with Korea. Well, good for him and good for America. Leonard was nothing if not a patriot. He was loyal, despite avoiding the draft, to both his country and his wife.

He hoped his dinner wouldn't surge up in his throat when he entered the front door, but he had high hopes of a speedy divorce. And the rain only served to reinforce his anger. The smell of the worms on the pavement caught in his throat. Worms were disgusting, and so was Lucy. And what was life for, anyway, if not to stand up for one's own rights, needs, and desires?

The worms on the front walk seemed to collude with his wife—they squirmed and looked pink and brown under the streetlamps like the tawny skin of her cheating face. But what if he'd been wrong about Lucy? He only *thought* she'd been unfaithful because a so-called friend had told him he'd "done" her months before, then toasted Leonard with a vodka-and-tonic in the bar where they'd had drinks. He'd seemed to exult in his "victory" over Leonard, who'd been such a faithful husband.

Leonard arrived at his own front door, the smell of the worms nearly asphyxiating him as he stood there, wondering what he would say to Lucy. She came to the entry just as he walked in, flush with the excitement of him finally—finally!, she thought—arriving home. How she'd missed him!

"Leonard! I have news!"

"News?" Leonard stood there in consternation. What could she possibly be about to tell him that could be good?

"And wonderful news it is—I'm pregnant!"

Leonard stood there, dripping from the September rain, not knowing whether to dismiss her on the spot or to celebrate. What had his friend been talking about, "doing" Lucy? Of course—he realized now—she couldn't ever have been unfaithful—and here she was, with their little Maltese cat winding its hungry path around her ankles, and she was smiling at him as if nothing had ever been wrong or come between them.

How he now regretted his solo dinner at the pub!—he should have come home to his loyal wife and eaten with her. He felt ashamed. And he suddenly felt filled with joy—the odor of the worms no longer bothered him, it was the month of September with autumn approaching, and all was right with the world. He was to be a father, and Eisenhower was turning out to be a good President, and the world was benevolent—except for his dastardly "friend"— and Lucy had always been kind and dedicated to him! How could he have been such a fool? He smiled and grabbed her by the waist, and wrapped her in his arms and kissed her, and thought, "I'll never be suspicious of her again."

He resolved in the future to unload such "friends" as his lying acquaintance had been. He was relieved and he was *home*.

###

THE DAMAGE DONE

I was young, a woman, and it was one of my first assignments after getting hired at *The Town Gazette*. It was a warm summer day and when she let me in she smiled a small smile, as if she was glad to have company. The small apartment was decorated with African statues and my hostess wore a green and yellow caftan. She apologized for the bandages on her wrists.

"I was in a car accident. My arms went through the window."

"I'm so sorry."

"Sit down. There's a glass of ice water."

"Thank you," I said, enjoying the ice against my tongue on that sultry summer day. My hostess curled up on the sofa, her legs tucked under her, her bare toes just peeping beneath the folds of her caftan. I pulled out my notebook, prepared to jot down anything significant, but was soon lost in her story.

"You can hardly imagine. You're a journalist with a promising career. And you come here to interview me about my father. Well, why wouldn't you? People wonder what a life like mine is like. I'll tell you. Yes, have another drink of water. I'm sorry, I've run out of coffee."

I set my notebook aside and resolved just to listen.

"He was a serial murderer. From the age of eleven I lived with this knowledge. But you already know that. And then when I got older, I watched friends walk down the aisle to get married, holding a father's arm. I knew I would never have that moment come. My father was in jail, for all the rest of his life. I lived like an ostrich, with my head down—how could I live with what my father did?—The callousness."

My hostess cleared her throat.

One victim was a textile worker—employed in a factory, nothing greater, nothing more than that. He was found, his skull smashed, arms tied behind his back, and he'd had a family of his own. An innocent who worked and did nothing to provoke my father."

She stroked the bandage on one of her wrists.

"I have received great love from friends who seem to understand my shame. They tell me I'm upstanding, a good and worthy person. They tell me I bring light to ordinary lives and not to be afraid. They tell me I'm a star shining in the dark. Does that sound naïve?"

My hostess got up from the sofa and began pacing around the room. She seemed distraught.

"Now, I hope I'll do good deeds one day for all Dad's victims—give a speech to people, or write a worthwhile book. Listen. I felt shame. When I was eleven, my mother told me Daddy was very sick and was going to prison. I felt as if I'd been struck with a hammer. People asked where Daddy was—I said he left to fight a war. How does one broach this topic? With fear and caution, shame."

She sat down again and I kept sipping my ice water. I hardly knew what to say.

"I have a memory...my father holding me on his big lap, when I was three. The loud TV was on and he laughed at the actors. A hard, coarse laugh—he didn't like these TV folk. Did I feel danger in his arms? No. Just wonder that he held me, feeding me a cookie... Excuse me. Are you hot?" she asked. I shook my head, not wanting to interrupt. "I can turn on the air conditioner if so. I don't use it much since I worry about the electric bill."

She rubbed her wrist.

"I saw him twice in prison...because I was still a child and I always wondered why he did it—rage? He felt righteous and so fair—they had "betrayed" him, exposed his low place in the world. His anger at other people was always justified, to him. I stopped answering his letters."

She picked up a little statue on the table next to her. It was carved out of wood and she played with it for a moment.

"You see me in this outfit, my styled hair, my manicure? I'm an attorney now, because I want some purpose in my life and I'm an advocate for children. I'm a realist. Trauma never ends,
but maybe I'm a very little star, emitting beams of hope with my tiny fistful of optimistic light."

She laid the statue down on the table and got up again.

"I'll let you go. That's all I have to say. Thanks for hearing me out."

I stood and walked with my glass of water to her kitchen and set it in the sink. Then I saw it—a razor blade, bloody, on the counter top. I realized she'd been cutting herself, and had only bandaged her wounds to shield me from that knowledge before I arrived.

I walked back into her living room and said goodbye, and she shook my hand.

I thought of calling for a medic when I left her place, but hadn't she already been through enough? And it was true that she'd bandaged the wounds. What was I supposed to do?

She'd been honest: trauma never ends, and even so she had goals and ambition. But I did wonder how much of an optimist she could be.

###

A FIELD OF POPPIES
(A Tale of the Vietnam War)

GARY (An American Ex-Soldier)

...Last night I dreamed I was in a field of poppies. But the poppies turned to blood. Everything was red around me. ...Good of you to come a hundred miles, Josh. Jeanne's away for the weekend. Nice to know my nephew doesn't mind keeping me company for a couple of days. Your cousin Alice is with your aunt. She would have liked to see you. But, well—girls' weekend away. ...I'm getting treatment...PTSD. Wake up with the sweats. Don't know how much longer Jeanne can take it. She says, "You were thrashing around all night last night." It frustrates her, but not as much as it frustrates me. You never fought, you don't know... Kids don't even demonstrate the way they used to, 'cause there's no draft. You're an innocent. What's it like to kill? I can tell you.

I was under orders. We captured him. Really, he was no more than a boy, either. I remember the terrified look on his face as I raised my gun to his head. ...Wish I had solid answers. People here at home try to help by asking questions. They ask if I feel guilt. Guilt? Not really. It's more like feeling sad, sad beyond words. It comes down to that, and that alone. Him or me. Who was going to have to go? No, I don't feel guilt. I was under orders. What I feel is enormous sadness. And fear of...the horror of it all.

Your cousin Alice's boyfriend is Vietnamese. Came to study here in America and stayed. Works in a dining commons at a university and buys a brand new car every two years. They have to, Vietnamese immigrants—they get ripped off by repairmen who know they don't speak English that well and charge them too much for a new transmission. So they buy a new car. ...I could help him not get ripped off. ...Do you know in Vietnam the average salary today is two dollars a day? So my daughter's boyfriend feels like a rich man in America. Alice might marry him. He's not so different from me, when I fell in love. Devoted to her. Only he's Vietnamese. A transplant. In America. With a job. And a car. He reminds me of that boy... My daughter keeps her distance from me. Doesn't want to know about all of it...the war. Anyway, that's all a man really wants, isn't it? A wife, a job, a car. You're 30 now, Josh—aren't those the things you want? ...But Jeanne says there's only so much she can listen to— see a doctor, she said. She's had enough. So I do see one—a psychiatrist. Can't say it doesn't help. He's a good doctor. And your Aunt Jeanne's a good wife. But they can't take away the horror. The doctor told me—suggested—that I keep a journal. I try, I write down my thoughts. But what good is it? I don't know. I'm no writer.

The memories—you become the best pal of those soldiers you're fighting with, and then, one day, it's all over. You're back in Spokane, or Dallas, or Fort Lauderdale. And hardly anyone thanks you for fighting for their country. At first. They do thank me now. But still, I wake up with nightmares. If I had it to do over… What would I have chosen instead? I was twenty. Didn't go to college. Thought I'd win a Purple Heart. The courage, the ignorance of a kid that age! …I wake up, middle of the night, in sweats and shakes. Because I can't forget his face. Once I tried to draw a picture of it—that fear, those Asian eyes, the memory of him. I thought I might find something of myself in the drawing. Something to make the two of us one, one whole person, instead of me just half a man. …Sadness. Not guilt. Guilt is for people who stayed at home. What I feel is an enormous, overwhelming sadness. And the recurring fear that there's something wrong that wasn't wrong with me before Vietnam.

*****

LY (A Vietnamese Woman)

My two roommates and I are looking for a fourth. We're quiet and we mind our own business, but we like having fun, too. You seem friendly and relaxed. My roommates and I cook together sometimes. They're Vietnamese, too. Do you think you'd like living with people like us? …You know, sometimes I miss where I came from. I grew up in the mountains. We were farming people. Even today I have calluses on my feet from going barefoot. Excuse me for putting lotion on my feet during our interview, but after all you'd be living with me and seeing it all the time. And my boyfriend—he's American—he thinks my feet are sexy!

I came to the US twenty years ago. Now my whole family lives here. My name, Ly, means "lion." And lions are strong and proud. I like thinking I am, too. I work in the dining commons of the university, checking students in to eat their meals. In the summers, when we get laid off for three months, I work as a chambermaid at a hotel. I take English lessons because I'm always trying to improve. I don't mind working hard. Oh, and if you're wondering, my American boyfriend never sleeps over. I go to his place. But maybe we'll get married someday and have a home together.

Do you know any of the history of my country? North Vietnam is the part the US dropped bombs on because we were Communist. Now our whole country is Communist. The Vietnamese are fighters; we don't give up easily. …Do you like bike riding? We ride bicycles at home. Many people don't have cars. I have a car now. I make good money. But do you know what it's like taking your car to a mechanic who charges too much for fixing it? It happens to me all the time, because I'm a foreigner.

These calluses. Women in America go to a salon to have them removed. But my boyfriend says they're a good thing. They mean I'm tough and strong. Except his sister says they're a sign of damage to the foot. She's nice. I've met her twice. My boyfriend took us out to dinner. I gave her a purse filled with makeup I got as a sample at one of those big department stores. ...In America people don't understand how it is to earn only two dollars a day. That's what I made at home. And Agent Orange—a horrible thing. Half a million children were born with birth defects because of it. It was called a "Rainbow Herbicide." And a rainbow is supposed to be a pretty thing. ...My whole family was affected by the war. But do you think I resent Americans too much? Don't think that. I came here because I wanted a richer life. And after all I am in love with one of your countrymen!

I got hurt in a car accident two years ago. The driver of the other car hit my car, so I went to a chiropractor for my back. The accident was in the country, near a field of poppies...I remember how red everything looked around me when I got hit. Like a very violent painting... My English was worse then. My American boyfriend helped translate when I went to my appointments. He's very considerate. ...Of course, I'm sorry I got hurt, and it's still a problem sometimes. And I miss my Vietnam, the hills, the farmland, the country. It's a beautiful place. I miss the food most of all. Sometimes I make fish soup with noodles. My boyfriend likes it. ...But I'm rambling, as you Americans say. I should tell you, we expect the rent paid the last day of each month. And we split the cost of household supplies. And we all have dinner together Sunday nights. So...do you think you'd like to move in?

*****

GHOST OF A VIETNAMESE BOY

He held the gun to my head. Terrible. I knelt on my knees in fear. I was trembling. I thought of my brothers and sisters, my mother. My cha, my bó, my father, who never wanted me to die this way. ...I thought of Canh Chua Ca, fish soup. I thought of the first girl I ever kissed. I thought of rain falling on the trees in Vietnam.

Strange being a ghost—like air, like being part of the wind, like nothing at all. And I have only memories to tide me over. I used to think when you died you were reborn—Buddhists believe this. And in school I read about Buddhism—a life beyond death—and Christianity, which speaks of eternal life. But I'm only a ghost, with a tale to tell.

I remember driving once through a field of white poppies—flowers as white as my garments—along the borders of Vietnam. They waved on their stalks in the breeze like women of the night calling out to us, as if to tempt me and the other passengers in the jeep. Poppies were used to make heroin. Comforting, consoling...sensations a soldier might value when he was asked to kill another man.

Why did it have to end this way? Youth interrupted. And maybe inconsequential, really.

I was only one of many. A bullet through my brain. He was shaking, himself. I won't forget his face—round-eyed, pale, an American. He looked afraid, too. He looked petrified. Isn't that what they say about wood that turns to stone? He suffered. Like Jesus on the cross, as I felt myself to be. ...I do not think anyone really wanted this war.

###

FATE

I've just been to see my neighbor. But I'm terribly nervous about the visit. Let me explain what happened...

I have a humble job as a schoolteacher and I'd heard this man was something of a crazed scientist. My wife suggested I go over to his place and introduce myself. Curious to meet him, I agreed and, since it's Saturday today, I knew we'd both be off for the weekend.

"Thanks for knocking on my door," he said, after I handed him a cake my wife had baked. "I like to know my neighbors, and since I just moved in, it's thoughtful making introductions. Thanks for the gift—I love pound cake! But you're not wearing a mask," he said.

"Forgot it. And I just tested negative."

"I'm not wearing one either. Don't believe in all that hoo-hah. And what's a little cough, anyway?" He coughed, a little laboriously, and I moved back a couple of feet from where he stood.

"Have a seat," he said, placing the cake on the coffee table. "I'm an amateur astrologist—

Let me bore you momentarily with my philosophy. I was just reading this book—," he stopped in mid-speech and held up a volume that was also on the coffee table, marked in the middle with a letter of some sort by which he was keeping his place.

"My sign is Cancer, born in summer," he went on. "Cancers love their homes—and their dear, beloved mothers. The sun and stars...just think! Would it be hell to know there's no free will regarding anything on earth?" He paused and peered at me through his thick glasses. "Maybe the Sun is the decision-maker, the God above to us mere men. My sign is always moon-ruled, and so— we get very weepy, dream a lot, and we are quite emotive creatures. And the big, mysterious Sun...well, what it may do to us is incredible..." He trailed off, then began coughing and wheezing again. "Do you follow me?"

"I'm just an elementary school teacher. I don't usually deal with such lofty concepts!" I laughed. "And I'm not much of a believer in fate."

"I'm a physics professor," he answered. "But I also believe in mystery. I'm a conundrum—even my students at the college don't understand me. Because in addition to the world of physics, I've also explored the *idea* of fate. The Sun. A mere great mass of gas and fire. But imagine it controls by math each last small thing, from foods you 'choose,' to trails of balls in pool halls that you've gladly struck at with a cue, or to the moment when you'll someday die?"

"Is it possible?" I wondered if he was quite sane.

"We all die. But who or what decides when?" he answered. "Here. Finish this beer. I just poured it out. Don't really feel like a Heineken right now. But it's a warm summer day and you ought to finish it for me. And yes, it's possible that the Sun controls us."

I gladly sipped the beer that was sitting on the coffee table. This strange new neighbor seemed to run off at the mouth a bit, but he was friendly.

"I never married," he continued. "But was that a choice? And did the Sun—or moon, my ruling planet—make me an agent of such bachelorhood? And was a wife just going to be more baggage? Look, I'm just a man who wonders at the universe's mystery. Make a toast with that beer!—that we can't predict the future—and perhaps the Sun protects us all from knowledge, lest we see too much! It's quite benevolent, our Sun. And when next you gaze at forces in our sky, you may reflect upon the mighty stars' control!"

And with that, believe it or not, he knelt on the floor and did a headstand! He must have been 50 and he was standing on his head. Then, just as suddenly, he relaxed and got back to his knees on the floor.

"There! Did the powerful Sun make me do a headstand? Or did I do it of my own free will?" He laughed. I thought he must be half-crocked and said I had to leave. But he stopped me.

"Just let me go to the bathroom quickly, and I'll pour you another beer. Keep me company. I like talking about philosophy." And with that, he excused himself to go to the bathroom and I was left in his parlor to poke around. There were two bookshelves, but not much other furniture except the sofa and an armchair, and there were dark green curtains over the windows that blocked out the sunlight—was he *afraid* of the sun?—and a little hallway that led to the kitchen. I picked up the astrology book he'd been reading and opened it to where he'd marked his place. The letter he'd used as a bookmark fell out onto the floor. Being a little nosy, I picked it up and unfolded it.

I'm not an alarmist, just normally careful. But what I read startled me beyond belief. It was a letter from his hospital saying he'd just tested positive for the coronavirus! And he wasn't even in isolation, and I'd shared his mug of beer! Had he exposed me to his germs on purpose? Was he that evil? Or was he just a nut?

I dropped the letter back into the book, replaced the book on the coffee table, and made my way to the door.

"Sorry—" I called out, almost yelling to him in the bathroom. "Got to leave. Can't stay any longer. And I really shouldn't have come anyway—safer not to associate with people these days—"

I fairly ran out of the house, slamming the door behind me, then ran down the sidewalk, and back to my own home where my wife was waiting for me. I was out of breath with excitement and anxiety.

"Call the doctor," I said to her in a rush. "I think I've been exposed to Covid!"

And now I'm a nervous wreck.

###

LIKE A DYNASTY

It was an odd sized casket, small. A flag was draped over it. It was carried by four men in uniform, though it was hard to tell for sure from a distance what uniform it was, or even if they were all men. There wasn't room for the usual six pallbearers due to the small size of the casket since it would have made for a comical service to have all six jammed together, shoulder-to-shoulder, crowding around an under-sized coffin. So the extra pallbearers were in the ranks of many others in uniform.

"Floyd lived well until death," said the Pastor. It seemed like a trite, stupid thing to say, but the fact was almost everyone there was crying, not least of whom was his mother, who wore a black lace dress and gold hoop earrings, and carried a purse decorated with jet beads, elegant though the family hadn't been rich. She looked like a tragic queen in her lace, with tears flowing from her eyes.

Floyd had died riding a motorcycle, but it was his service in Afghanistan that he was really being remembered for. He'd enlisted because he didn't know what to do after high school, and maybe service was a ticket to a college education. He'd served two years. I recall him telling our second grade class that his father read **Playboy** and that his mother was a hairdresser. I suppose you would have called them working class.

But it was actually the motorcycle I remembered most. I'd grown up with Floyd, in the same class, and recalled his long, silky blond hair and chipped front tooth when I'd seen him at a graduation party at the end of twelfth grade. He wasn't tall; only about five feet seven inches, and he was slender. He was dating Wendy, a girl who was overweight but who had a sunny personality, and everyone liked her.

Floyd bought the Honda used, and rode it every day to school. When my own brother bought a motorcycle, too, my mother was unbelievably alarmed and went into the yard as Ronnie started up the engine, grabbed the handlebars and tried to wrestle the bike away from him. Perhaps she had a premonition of what would happen to Floyd. I don't know. But Ronnie took off on the bike, and then, three years later, Floyd died on his own "wheels."

My mother came to me in my bedroom that awful night, after Floyd had returned from the war, and banged on the door, and fairly shouted at me that Floyd had just been killed. It was almost as if she were blaming *me*—though of course I had nothing to do with it. And my brother Ronnie had long since sold his own motorcycle, and bought a more sensible four-door sedan instead to ferry his boyfriend around in.

When Floyd died I was heartbroken. I'd had a crush on him in high school, and when he fell in love with Wendy it just about killed me. But Wendy was an optimist and a cheery type, and I've always been rather solitary and even surly in disposition. My mother still calls me a "crank" and says I need to learn to be more agreeable.

When Floyd went off to war, a lot of people didn't think he should have. We came from Massachusetts, where many people are liberals, and a lot of them disagreed with sending more troops to Afghanistan. But that's what Floyd wanted, I guess—to be a real soldier. He got his long hair cut before he left and I remember him telling me he hoped to return a hero. But all of this is almost ancient history now.

Three days after the motorcycle accident was the memorial service. Wendy was there, of course, but she didn't speak—that was left to Floyd's father, who stood so steady and upright, like a king in his grief, almost, and his older brother, and a couple of friends of Floyd's from high school, and of course a few soldiers Floyd had known in the war. . They all said how loyal and trustworthy Floyd had been. His father told a story about how when he'd been five Floyd had stolen a candy bar from the drug store, and when his mother discovered the theft and made him return the candy, Floyd cried and apologized to the owner of the store as if he'd brought terrible shame on them all.

Everyone at the service chuckled at this story, for they all knew how emotional Floyd had been, even as a little boy. His mother told me after the service that Floyd had never once forgotten to give her roses on Mother's Day and a bottle of Fracas perfume for Christmas. He was that kind of son, loving and reliable and sentimental about holidays.

But what struck me most was something else his mother said to me just before she turned away to go home with her husband. She had tears running down her face and was clutching her beaded purse with anxious hands. She leaned in towards me, so close that she seemed to be whispering. She was obviously overwrought.

"You know," she said to me confidentially, "I believe you knew Floyd as well as any of his friends, but did you know he was secretly gay? I'd known from the time he was ten. That long blond hair—he reminded me of a little girl. And I'd always wanted a little girl. Anyway, he told me when he got back from Afghanistan that he was gay and had had a love affair with another soldier while in the service."

She was almost choking on her words. I wondered if, later, she'd regret having confided in me. Truth be told, I'd never known this and always thought Floyd reserved his deepest love for Wendy. I wondered if even **she** knew. But

Wendy was standing apart from us with some acquaintances from high school, and I didn't think she could have known, since she'd always seemed so devoted to Floyd. Floyd's mother touched my arm.

"I'm only telling you because I know your own brother Ronnie's gay," she said. It was true, my brother had come out a year earlier and was working for gay social justice for a city political action committee. But I hardly knew what to say after Floyd's mother had told me Floyd was gay, too. Had Ronnie known? He and Floyd were never close.

"I didn't know about Floyd," I said to his mother. "But I'm sure he brought you lots of joy and that you were very proud of him." They seemed like lame words; I didn't think I'd spoken very eloquently to her. But she smiled at me and wiped her tears away with her hand. She said "thank you," and I was casting about for what to say before the casket was lowered into the grave.

At that moment Wendy approached us. She grabbed Floyd's mother's hand and told her what a lovely speech Floyd's father had made. She was crying, too, and I kept wondering how Floyd could have kept up the charade of loving Wendy when he'd had a romance with a man in Afghanistan. My brother Ronnie had never even pretended to have a girlfriend.

But Wendy surprised me. She stroked Floyd's mother's hand between her own two hands and spoke vehemently, as if she was relieving herself of a big secret she'd held in for years. She, too, was almost choking on her words and she kept glancing at me warmly as if we were old pals, even though we never really were. She looked like a princess in her flowing dress, although she was somewhat heavy, because she'd worn a tiny little tiara over her flowing dark hair that she told me Floyd had bought her while in Afghanistan. He'd remembered to bring something back for her, and it was a tiara worthy of royalty!

"You might not know—or probably by now you do—but he was gay," she said to Floyd's mother. "He told me our senior year, but he also said he loved me and could possibly swing both ways. He asked me to marry him once he got back from Afghanistan, but of course how could I do that? I'd have been jealous of other **men**. And, honestly, we never slept together. It was a teen romance but there was never anything physical about it, between us, I mean."

I was surprised she was telling me and Floyd's mother all this. I also wondered if it relieved Floyd's mother that he'd apparently been bi-sexual, not just out-and-out gay, because she'd seemed distressed about what she'd been telling me. After a moment, Floyd's mother and I walked away, waiting for the actual burial. Floyd's mother kissed Wendy on the cheek when they parted, then asked me if I'd be needing a ride home later. But I told her I'd come with my parents, who had disappeared from view—I knew I'd catch up with them before we left the cemetery.

The grave wasn't ready until sunset, so the whole event was rushed and disorganized, except for the very last part. The grave was a massive affair, more of a crater than a grave, and it took until dark to roll the casket down to the bottom. If any prayers were said, they couldn't be heard over the dull thudding of the clods raining down on the casket far below.

###

THE SILVER-TONGUED DEVIL

Lily is 38, a former actress from New York who is now a writer. She is young-spirited, young-looking, emotional, introspective, and wears beautiful clothing. Mark, 40, is her lover, a successful painter, dark and good-looking, an expert listener, and spends a great deal of time talking with her. He has an easy, smooth manner and is careful in what he says. He has an air of bravado about him, although he passes well for a gentleman.

The scene is a Victorian bedroom not far from the waterfront in a hotel in Boston in the year 1899. There is a brass bed, an end table, and a side table with two chairs beside it. Two glasses and an open bottle of red wine are placed on the side table. There is also a mirror, and a coat rack and two valises near the door. Mark is lying on the unmade bed, asleep. The sound of the whistle from a steam locomotive comes in through the window from time to time.

Lily is standing at the end table near the bed, counting out her money. She counts it—three hundred dollars—twice, and lays the money down and crosses to the window and looks out. She puts her hands on her waist and heaves a big sigh.

"At last!" She sighs again, and then laughs. She turns and crosses to her valise and pulls out a feathered harlequin mask. She toys with it in her hands, then crosses to the mirror, with the mask covering her eyes, and looks at herself. She laughs again.

Then she crosses to the bed and lies down, leaning over Mark with the mask still held before her eyes.

"Wake up, sleepyhead!"

She ruffles the feathers on the mask against Mark's cheek. He opens his eyes, wraps his arms around her, and kisses her.

"You little vixen! Where did you get that mask?"

"I brought it with me. It's from the old days."

"Ah."

"Oh, Mark—I'm so happy right now!" Mark sits up in the bed.

"And why?"

"Because of you. And us. And I'm happy for the present."

"I am as well." Mark smiles.

"Funny how things change—" Lily lays the mask down on the end table. "Life is so amazing." Mark laughs.

"And what's so amazing to you about this—here, now?"

"Do you really take so much for granted?" Lily sighs with impatience.

"I just wonder what's got you in such a—mood!"

"Well, we took the train together from New York to come up here to Boston," Lily continues, "and we're on a holiday, and that's a good, new beginning, and—I have a little income now. And I have you. And you have income, too. Rather a lot. And all of that makes me happy." Mark rubs his eyes, still sleepy.

"And you've woken me out of a sound sleep to tell me that?"

Lily smiles.

"You can't be asleep in the middle of the afternoon when I'm not!" She frowns suddenly.

"Mark. I've been thinking. About money. And love."

"Money is a lovely thing."

"…And how much I needed both at one time. I feel as if I'm taking advantage of you. I know you can afford to support me, but really—"

"Lily, I don't mind."

"I know, but maybe that's why I don't feel very modern compared to other women. I need to write. I need to write novels."

They are now lying side-by-side, sideways across the bed.

"I like being your source of comfort," answers Mark. "People everywhere are buying my paintings. I'm proud to take care of you. And maybe someday you can take care of me!"

Lily peers at him closely.

"Yes, but you see, I had a very hard time for a while. I made a bad bargain." She lights a cigarette from the end table. "I apologize I never told you until now. It's just that the story is so sad."

"Tell me," says Mark.

Lily pauses for a moment.

"I used to be an actress. I lived in a room with very little furniture, and little food. I was thin, I had no pretty clothes. I had nothing, really, except what my family sent me."

"An actress? I never guessed. So you 'trod the boards'!!!"

Lily continues.

"Oh, I know actresses are thought of as whores, but I never thought of them that way. I thought the acting world created magic, that actors created dreams. And I wanted success so badly. I've always loved watching people on stage, people who are talented at what they do, who make the world a more beautiful place. They matter to me. And I really was talented. I'd had good notices in the papers. Actor-managers told me I was good. Gentlemen friends told me."

Mark is a bit impatient.

"Yes, you were good. I believe you. Go on."

"Are you sure you want to hear? It gets worse. One day I realized I'd lost whatever I had as an actress. Here's the hard part. I made the mistake of falling for a man, giving him everything I had, emotionally, and then, well…. we had a very bad parting and I had nothing left. I felt dried up, devoid of a self. I felt empty. Do you understand?"

Mark laughs.

"Yes. I struggled as a painter for many years. And many women have broken my heart. I understand. One becomes frustrated being relegated to the ranks of the untalented. Despair sets in."

Lily puts out her cigarette.

"But I hadn't been untalented—before that. And I wasn't really, afterwards, either. Years later, it came over me one day—I'm telling you a secret—one day I realized I was successful, at something I never thought I'd do. Not at acting, but at writing. At pouring out my soul on paper. Only it wasn't good news, after all. It was scary."

Mark responds casually.

"What happened?"

"Well, after falling in love with this poet, I wrote a letter to him making up for the way we'd parted."

"He was a poet?"

"A successful one. But he was married, and besides he had too many other women in his life."

"So you got smart and left him. That takes courage."

"—and I never heard from him again, only in the poetry he published, and it was all so strange and inexplicable, how he began writing about me without us ever being together again. Except that one day I thought I saw his carriage outside my building. I thought he called to me, but I wasn't sure it was him and, in any case, I was too tired and distraught to answer. I hadn't slept well in months. He'd affected me. But then, this is the odd part—a couple of years later I realized everybody around me seemed to know who I was. I didn't know why strangers who must have known this fellow were being so eccentric and rude to me. You see, this poet, after I wrote to him, wanted to see me again after all."

Mark clears his throat and seems impatient again.

"Hmmm. What makes you so sure?"

"Because I had written him such a passionate letter. A lyrical letter, full of rage and sentiment and nostalgia. And he showed my letter around, I know he did. He passed it along to his friends. Anyway, it seems I'd developed a reputation for being a femme fatale. Because strangers were acting so impolite around me. I felt like a pariah. And after a while I felt as though I were losing my mind."

There is a sudden banging on the door from the Concierge of the ho tel. Mark risesand opens the door.

"Yes? What is it?"

The Concierge groans.

"Sir and Madam, I must ask, you've eaten at the hotel these past three days and charged it to your room, but you must pay now! I don't know you, I don't know if you'll pay the bill."

Lily exclaims loudly.

"My goodness, we're guests here! Do you always treat your visitors this way?"

The Concierge responds in kind.

"I must receive payment for the food! The bill for the room—that must be settled, too."

"Well, of course, it will be." Lily takes 30 dollars out of her pocketbook on the end table and hands it to the Concierge. "Here. Will that cover the food?"

"Yes. And how long do you and the gentleman plan to stay?"

"I don't know."

"Other customers may want accommodation."

"We'll pay for the room today. We'll be down to the front desk shortly. And now you'll leave us in peace?"

"But of course, Madam." The Concierge bows and exits.

"My God," says Lily to Mark. "Even here, in Boston, people are eager to see one "ante up." I thought we had solitude and quiet here."

"Well, you've paid for the food. Thank you. I didn't bring much money with me."

Lily smiles.

"Aha! You're practically being kept by me, Mark! And you've told me how successful you are!" But Mark challenges her.

"You accuse me of boasting?!"

"Not at all. And yet—" She smiles again. "You're a very charming man but you must have been lying! At least a little…"

"I didn't know how long we'd stay in Boston…"

"It's all right. We'll stay as long as we like. But I was telling you about this man."

"He must have been a brute! I don't understand. What did you write to this poet that made him decide to see you again? And what was so wonderful about him?"

Lily thinks for a second.

"Well, to begin with, his friends had ganged up on me earlier. They followed me into a tavern one night and berated me. It was because I hadn't slept with him. I've told you, he was married. They said I thought I was too attractive for him, and asked did I want to be beaten and abused, did I want to be violated? They thought I must be in pursuit of another man. And they wondered who was I to lead him on—someone like him?"

"You should have gone to the police."

But Lily waves her hand in dismissal.

"Oh, you can't go to the police for idle threats. Anyway, I wrote to the married poet. The letter was very dramatic. I ended it with a quotation from Rimbaud. It was the closing line from 'A Season in Hell.'"

The whistle from a steam locomotive is heard through the window. Lily goes on.

"It was published in France, in 1873. Have you never read the poem? Rimbaud is writing about his relationship with Verlaine, another male poet. They were lovers."

Mark scoffs.

"Homosexuals?"

"Yes," answers Lily. "It's not such a terrible thing as all that—anyway, 'A Season in Hell' was about their relationship. It's so passionate! And in part of the poem Rimbaud writes from the point of view of a woman."

"Hmph!"

"He tells of being surrounded by Demons—characters who drive one mad. And Rimbaud closes with the line—it brings a chill to me even now—'I saw the Hell of women back there, and I shall be free to possess Truth in one soul and one body.'" Rising off the bed, Lily starts pacing around the room. "It's a prediction, that last line."

"Meaning you two would be together again?" Mark is annoyed.

"Either that, or that I might spend the rest of my life alone. I wonder if he was as struck by that line as I was—"

"Maybe. You must have meant something quite special to him."

"Oh, but it was never right between us. He was a roué, he fancied other women, and I was a sensitive young girl who probably read far too much for her own good!"

"Lily, you're pacing," says Mark. "You do that a lot. Learn to calm yourself."

Lily stops pacing.

"I didn't know what to do—I couldn't retract my letter. And it appeared the gossip had spread. Because he wanted me back, and I didn't go back to him. Tell me what you think about all of this. I'm dying to know."

Mark lights a cigarette.

"Well, it's all over now and you can't go back. That's what I think. Tell me more about this poet. Who was he?"

"Do you really want to know? He was famous, and he wore tight trousers and had lots of lady followers and many colorful poet friends, but he had an angry temper and I probably shouldn't have fallen for him, but he made my world exciting. I felt romantic with him. He had a silver tongue. And he was a bohemian."

Mark is irritated again.

"I don't want to hear about him," Mark says with some bravado. "Trust me, I'm a better man than he was!"

Lily ignores what Mark has said.

"The letter I'd written was too much, you see. It was so personal, as though I'd handed him the very means by which to drive a spike through my heart, since he wrote about me later. And perhaps I'd done the very same thing to him, driven a spike through his heart, just by sending a letter."

"This is all nonsense," Mark sputters. "And you should forget it. You torture yourself too much."

"Maybe I do." Lily pauses again. She crosses to the table in the corner, pours herself a glass of wine, and sits in one of the armchairs. "And then his wife divorced him, for adultery and abandonment. Because my letter had been circulated, spread around. It was a scandal. She must have known he'd had other women…maybe a divorce was in the cards anyway, but I was the catalyst."

"So you felt guilty…and ashamed, probably. But it was his own fault. You didn't do anything to cause it."

Lily objects.

"I felt I had. I felt dishonored. I was wretched…And in the end I never returned to him. Anyway, afterwards my life was different. People behaved as if they had knowledge and authority over me and treated me as though I were familiar to them. I was miserable. I cut my arteries open with a razor, which is why I have scars to this day."

Mark glares at her.

"My God," he says. "I wondered about those, but I didn't want to presume anything. I assumed you'd had a hard time in your youth. This is a very complicated story." Then he laughs. "Christ! How I would love to receive a letter like the one you wrote!"

"You wouldn't."

"I would. To have a woman nearly die for me!"

"That's insanity." Lily is aggravated.

"No, it's love."

"How can you be so crude as to wish for that?"

But Mark slaps her, and she cries out.

"For your own good I did that," he says. "Be intelligent. Come to terms with what happened. We've all known misery."

"That was an awful thing to do, what you just did."

"I'm sorry. I just can't stand to see you worrying so much about the past. I apologize."

"You're callous sometimes, you know that?"

"I said I was sorry."

"I'll only forgive you if you listen."

"Ah, Lily, I'll listen long into the night! We're here together, now, in this moment, and isn't it all wonderful? Tell me more about your life. But not about this poet."

"You don't understand. He affected me for years. A married man. And he betrayed my privacy. But he probably felt justified showing my letter around. I'm still not sure why I cared so much. Anyway, that was a long time ago, and I was rescued from suicide, and now I'm writing, I'm not acting in the theatre anymore. And I'm lying on this bed with you on a holiday in Boston, and nobody knows where I am, and in an hour we'll get up and walk along the waterfront, and then we'll change our clothes and go have dinner somewhere, and we'll come back to our room at this hotel, and have romance…"

Mark crosses to the other armchair.

"I knew you were sad a few months ago," he says, "I just didn't know why. The scars are nothing." He pauses while he pours himself a glass of wine, then speaks a bit jovially. "Put the past behind you."

Suddenly the Maid knocks. Lily opens the door and speaks.

"I told the Concierge we'd be down shortly."

The Maid speaks hesitantly.

"Oh, but—"

Mark is angry.

"What's the matter? Must we constantly be interrupted?"

"I'm sorry Sir, and Miss. I just need to make up your bed with fresh linen."

Lily is kind.

"Well. Go ahead."

The Maid proceeds to make up the bed. Lily turns to Mark.

"At any rate, you've heard my tale of woe."

Mark sighs.

"People are stupid and cruel, Lily. There are people who would as soon pick your pocket as smile at you. Let me tell you a story. Maybe you'll find this, about my own past, interesting. I've never told you before because it's embarrassing. But I'm proud of how it turned out." He takes a sip of wine and looks at the Maid. The Maid is apologetic again.

"Would you rather I leave, Sir?"

"No. You're a clever, nice young girl. I'm just filling my friend in on how I turned the tables on someone." He addresses Lily. "Many years ago I was an apprentice to a famous painter. I filled in sketches he rendered with the colors he directed me to, and I finished paintings he didn't have time to complete."

Lily exclaims enthusiastically.

"I love hearing about your work!"

Mark continues.

"But listen. One day a rich man came into his studio to see this painter's canvases. And this man looked around the studio for a long time, trying to select just the right painting to take back to Europe with him. At last he settled on one of mine. Oh, it was signed by my employer, but I did all the work on it. And, since my employer was not in the studio to tell him, I explained to the visitor that most of the work on the painting was mine."

Lily interrupts.

"Good for you. You told the truth."

Mark goes on with his story.

"I didn't want him to think that he was buying a true original of this famous painter's. Just then my employer returned to the studio. Pleased that he had an interested buyer, he told the man that the painting was thoroughly a work of his own, that no one else had had a hand in it. He wanted badly to sell something, as he'd gotten down on his luck in recent months." Mark takes another sip of wine and goes on.

"'It can't be true,' the buyer said. He challenged him. 'The painting obviously can't be an original, because this young man just told me otherwise.'" Mark stands. "Offended, my employer sent me out of the room. I discovered later that a sale was never made. And my employer told me, after the visitor left, accusing him of untruthfulness, that I could no longer work there." Mark paces. "'You're finished!' he said."

"Oh, how awful!" says Lily. "You were only trying to protect him!"

"Yes, but he was furious. And over the next few months I could find nobody who would hire me, because this painter spread the word that I had been a greedy, dishonest apprentice. I was shattered. But I started working on my own. I borrowed money to set up my own studio, and after a year I sold three paintings. And I learned that I was good enough to do it! I hadn't thought I was talented enough to try."

Lily interrupts again.

"But of course you were!"

Mark is proud.

"So I'm telling you, Lily, based on my own hard-won experience, that you need to ignore the past, because the only thing that really matters now is the present and the future. This poet you knew sounds like a bastard. And if things hadn't happened the way they did, you and I never would have met. So I propose that you accept whatever good came out of it and from now on ignore the rest. ...I'm a little jealous of this man you loved so many years ago. You know, I met a young actress once who was much like you, except that she took opium to calm her nerves. Mind you, I'm not recommending it."

The Maid stops her work and looks at Mark, startled. Lily laughs.

"I don't take opium! Anyway, I can see you've suffered too." She pauses and thinks for a moment. "You know, I really don't miss acting at all. I'm writing novels now and that's how I satisfy my ambitions. I know women don't tend to make a success of themselves that way. It's usually men who do, but.... Oh, Mark! I value your friendship and esteem so much. You listen to me."

The Maid finishes her work and exits. Mark crouches next to Lily and puts his hand under her chin.

"Lily, you're my Muse. I love to paint you." He stands and moves behind her chair. She kisses the hand he has placed on her shoulder, then drinks from her glass of wine.

"We're two artists. We're good for each other. Oh, Mark! I'm so sorry for so much I've done! I made such a disastrous muddle of things! But I'm wiser now. I know the depths of the human soul. And I can forgive, maybe not myself, but certainly the people I've known."

"But you should forgive yourself!"

Lily crosses back to the bed, wipes her eyes, then stretches her arms over her head and lies down.

"I've been trying. Don't tell me, I know: just because life is terrible for ten years doesn't mean it has to be forever. It can change, the tide turns, it's like the sun rising after a terrible storm, and nobody can stop it from happening!"

There is another banging on the door from the Concierge.

"Sir and Madam—we must have you come down to pay for the room.

Right now!"

Mark groans.

"Oh, for Heaven's sake!"

"I can't have this!," says the Concierge through the door. "Three days you've been at this hotel and where's the money for the room? I'm getting old; I can't keep climbing these stairs to remind you. I have grandchildren who have to eat. Some consideration, please!"

Lily calls out.

"We're coming down now."

Mark reprimands Lily.

"This was a terrible place to stay. You can hear the trains rolling through constantly."

"I'm sorry, Mark."

Lily calls through the door.

"...Yes, yes, we'll come down and pay right away. And now please leave us alone." The Concierge leaves. Lily reaches for her pocketbook, on the bedside table and takes money out.

"Look. I've got three hundred dollars as an advance for my next novel. We can use it to pay the hotel bill! I want to."

Mark crosses to her on the bed and lies down next to her again.

"Well, if you insist. Though I'd rather I paid—Anyway, you deserve to do what you like. We both do." He kisses her. "Life's a miracle, Lily." He puts his hand on her breast, and tries to kiss her again. She pushes his hand away.

"I know. I've been saved by accident too many times not to believe it."

"It's no accident," he goes on. "It's art. And it's design. Look, Lily. We're passionate people. We've both endured bad reputations. But you're a lovely woman, with a heart and a brain, and can't you see that everything that happened is simply what was meant to be? And we're lying here, a few hundred yards from the waterfront, with the sun shining through the window, and our hearts are beating together at this moment in time, and it's the start of a new century—that's design, too. It's not an accident. We were meant to be together this way."

"Oh, Mark—you have a silver tongue! You know just what to say!"

"I told you, I'm a better man than any poet you ever knew!" He tries to unbutton her bodice, and again she pushes his hand away. "You're rejecting me." He sounds insulted. Suddenly he twists her arm behind her back. "I want you. Now."

Lily is offended.

"Don't be so abrupt. This isn't the right time—I need to think."

"If not now, then when??"

"Later. Mark! You're hurting me!"

"You're a tease." Mark speaks sharply.

"That wasn't my intention."

"Don't be coy. A man needs his pleasure, too."

Lily twists away from him.

"Let me go!"

"I'm only being playful." He relinquishes his hold on her. "You need to comport yourself. This isn't all about you. And life isn't just about conversation."

"I don't feel in the mood right now. Really, you're too rough. I needed to talk today. Can't you understand? It's all right for you. You may never have found, and then lost, a love in such a disturbing way."

"Of course I have. Everyone has. Look. What you think and what you feel may be of paramount importance to you, but it matters little to the average man on the street."

Lily objects.

"But we're not average people."

Marks sighs again.

"No. I hope to God not."

Lily goes on.

"You know, I used to believe I was nothing. But now I know that's not true. Everything's all turned around. I can feel my heart beating again, and it's been so long! If I weren't so tired, I'd cry again. And now…" She rolls over onto her back. "Let's go to sleep. After I pay the bill. And I will go down in a minute to pay it. But I want to dream. I want to be unconscious, and I want to forget. So hold me. Help me put my fears back into a little tiny box, and help me live again. That's all that matters. To be alive in the moment into which one is born. Do you understand?" She is falling asleep. "Hold me. Now and forever. Just hold me."

"I will." Mark puts his arm around her comfortingly. "My angel. My actress. My writer."

Lily smiles in her exhaustion.

"My painter. My artist. My one true friend," she says. They kiss and Lily falls asleep. There is a long pause. Mark stares at her. He thinks for a moment, and then slowly, trying to be quiet, rises from the bed. He delivers his next speech while he is putting on his cravat, which is draped over one of the chairs, and his coat, hung on the coat rack.

"Your one true friend? Your one true friend? I'll bet you've had many. You're pretty, and talented. Oh, Lily. I will not be here when you awaken. I'm sorry, but I can't bear your whining and complaining. You, with your sad tales of forgotten loves and letters bandied about and what you think of as 'honor.' You make me jealous. Don't you think I've suffered just as much to get where I am? I'd be ashamed if I were you." He adjusts his cuffs and cufflinks. "I won't take care of you. Forgive me if you can, but I can't think of you as anything but a woman who's starved for attention. I'm sorry. I won't soon forget you." He takes up his hat from the coat rack. "But I'm sick of infamy, of shame. I want only happiness from this petty life. I want to live unemcumbered by a female who has all the rationality of a madwoman!"

With a last look at Lily, sleeping on the bed, he takes the 300 dollars off the bedside table and puts it in his pocket, then picks up his walking stick that is leaning against the coat rack.

"Good-bye! I'm taking the train to New York."

Lily suddenly become alert and rises off the bed.

"Mark! Damn you! Leave the money. I'd hate to have to call in the police."

Mark stutters.

"I—I thought you were—"

"Asleep? I seldom fall asleep these days. Put it back."

Mark puts the money where he found it.

"You're a scoundrel! I've poured out my heart to you, and you take me so cheap!"

Mark scoffs in disgust.

"You don't know how good you have it. You wanted to win my sympathy. My hand in marriage, maybe. You've used me as much as I ever used you. It was a game!"

"No, it wasn't, it wasn't at all," says Lily, "but I believe it was to you. I wouldn't marry you now if you were the last man on earth. I tell the truth. You didn't. I could see it in your eyes. You were bored. You were ready to leave as soon as you possibly could. To take my money, to abandon me, to make a hasty exit and leave on the very next train. And except for the money, now I hope you will."

Mark looks at her with scorn.

"You pity yourself too much."

"And you're a coward. My words fell on deaf ears."

"Someday you'll write to me," Mark continues, "and do you know what will happen? I won't answer."

"Don't hold your breath. Should we meet on the street, I wouldn't speak to you at all. I'll never write to you. You can offer me nothing now."

"You're a bitch!" says Mark.

"And you're awful!" responds Lily. But Mark won't shut up.

"…Wasting my time, telling me things I never wanted to hear." He spits at her, then picks up his valise that is near the door, and leaves.

Lily thinks for a moment.

"What a demon! He's gone. Thank God." She lights a cigarette and smokes as she paces around the room, then puts the cigarette out. She takes out a tablet, a quill pen, and a bottle of ink from her valise near the door. The Maid knocks. Lily opens the door.

"I'm sorry, Miss. I forgot to clear the wine glasses."

Lily is relieved to see her.

"Come in. You did a very good job making up the bed."

"I'm glad." The Maid takes the wine glasses from the table and puts two others in their place. She speaks hesitantly. "Will the gentleman be coming back very soon?"

Lily doesn't reply.

"May I confide in you, Miss?"

Lily is surprised at this little maid.

"Of course."

The Maid speaks haltingly.

"I just thought—you seem such a lady. …I had a man once. Well, I suppose he was really only a boy. He was eighteen, I was a year younger. He worked as an assistant to a prominent lawyer. I thought I'd marry him. But it never did work out. He fell in love with someone else."

"Really? How old are you now?"

"Just nineteen."

"Still young," says Lily. "So. You're well rid of him."

"Thank you. This boy—I hardly think of him anymore. I'm better off now." She replaces the cork into the wine bottle and wipes the bottle with her apron. "I'm nothing, I know. My life is hard. But you seem to be so—such a lady." She trails off. "I wanted to ask you, Miss. Is this man of yours nice? He seemed that way. I just wondered. I don't know much about gentlemen."

Lily thinks for a moment.

"No. I don't believe he is nice."

"But you keep company together."

"Not any more, I'm afraid." Lily puts her hand to her forehead as if she is about to faint. "And I'm not feeling well."

"Oh, Miss! Is there anything I can do?"

Lily recovers. She takes money from the table and hands it to the Maid.

"I'll be all right. Give this to the Concierge. You know, you remind me of myself a few years ago. I was as gullible as you, and maybe I still am."

The Maid nods respectfully.

"People do tell me I am naïve."

"Yes. It's not good to be naïve. You should know, my little friend, that you can't trust anyone who only 'seems' like a gentleman."

The Maid looks at the money in her hand.

"You trust me."

"I do. Because you're young, and sweet, and you earn an honest living."

"Thank you, Miss. You're very kind. If you're sure there's nothing else I can do, I'll go now." She curtseys and departs.

"Goodbye," says Lily, then speaks to herself. "Hmph! Life is so odd sometimes. Friends turn out to be strangers, and strangers friends." She looks out the window. "And just today I was wondering what to write about next. My new novel. Now I know how to begin."

She sits in one of the armchairs at the side table, picks up her pen, dips it into the ink,
and begins writing, talking as she writes.

"It's a warm, spring afternoon. A woman and a man are lying on a bed. 'Mark,' she says to him, 'I really feel as if I'm taking advantage of you. I know you can afford to support me, but really—'"

The sound of a locomotive is heard again, and Lily continues to write as if possessed by her newfound love, ink on paper.

###

THE AFFAIRS OF THE RICH

"I write this will entirely disinheriting my oldest son, for reasons he well knows."

With that, as a legal secretary at a Jewish law firm in New York, I typed the opening paragraph of a will written by Joseph Weinberg, dated January 2000, just before the coronavirus struck in full force. I'd been working at the firm for three months, happily, and my bosses were kind and considerate.

In May, I found out from one of my bosses that Joseph had died of COVID in the hospital. He'd been put on a ventilator, but it didn't help him survive. I kept thinking about the will I'd typed not long before his death, and what the reasons for his sternness were.

It bothered me, his will—why had he disinherited his oldest son, and what if his oldest son, named Jacob, didn't really know why he'd been disinherited?

That afternoon in May, after finding out Joseph had died, I went shopping for lace stockings with a co-worker at a little store on the ground floor of the Empire State Building. It was our lunch hour and we wanted some relief and fun. While at the cashier's desk in the front of the store, we were preceded by two elderly women who were buying souvenirs—keychains and little statues of the Empire State Building—and were talking to each other. I couldn't help overhearing, and got an answer to my questions about the mysterious Joseph who had written such an angry will.

"Joseph Weinberg, my husband," said one of the gray-haired ladies at the register, "was a nut. When he died two weeks ago I wasn't terribly sorry to lose him. Of course, the virus is awful, and I did visit him behind a glass partition in the hospital, but he was always unkind to my oldest, Jacob."

I was stunned. Could this possibly be the wife of the man whose will I'd typed in January, and could she possibly be explaining to her New York friend why he'd bailed out on his son? But apparently she was.

"Awfully ungenerous of him," said her companion, and she laid her credit card on the cashier's counter top.

"You said it," said the woman who I assumed was Mrs. Weinberg. "He never forgave Jacob for converting. Jacob married Ellen two years ago, who came from a strict Catholic family. And even though Jacob wanted their children raised Jewish, like us, Ellen insisted they be raised Catholic and go to Mass and celebrate Christmas with her family."

"Oh, my," said Mrs. Weinberg's companion. "How stressful for your husband. When my own son, Caleb, married, his Protestant wife agreed to raise the kids Jewish."

"But that's just the least of it," said Mrs. Weinberg. "Ellen's grandfather was a Nazi soldier in Germany. And she seemed to have some sympathy for him, since she kept his old uniform in a closet in their house."

"A Nazi soldier? Her grandfather? That's something to be ashamed of!" said Mrs. Weinberg's friend.

"Yes, but Ellen didn't agree. She thinks Jews have caused much misery to the world and doesn't ever want the kids to go to temple or celebrate Yom Kippur or Rosh Hashanah or any other Jewish holidays."

"Then why did she marry Jacob?" asked the friend.

My co-worker was getting impatient waiting for these customers to finish at the register, and just then said, "Let's forget buying these stockings. We have to get back to the office."

But I wanted to hear the end of Mrs. Weinberg's story. So my co-worker and I stood there, waiting to make our purchases. Mrs. Weinberg continued.

"And so Joseph disinherited Jacob. And Joseph was worth five million. I've often wondered if he had regrets as he was dying, because Jacob has always been the most attentive to him and also the most religious child in our family. When he fell in love with Ellen, whose grandfather was a Nazi, I could hardly believe it. But Jacob told me she'd also sided with her grandmother when she'd been tried for murdering her husband, the Nazi sympathizer who'd been unfaithful to her. She, too, was Catholic."

"What strange marriages you have in your family—so much religious discord," said the friend. "And a trial for murder?"

"Yes, but the grandmother was exonerated. She never committed the murder. Her husband had already had a child with the other woman, and the jury sympathized with the grandmother. Unusual for a woman to be exonerated for murder, given that day and age, when married women weren't often supported by the law. Her husband's death was discovered to be caused by a burglar in their home."

At that point, my co-worker finally gave up waiting to pay for her purchases, returned her stockings to the rack, and said she was going back to the office so as not to be late. But I kept waiting, wanting to hear the end of this woman's story, whose husband's will I'd typed months earlier.

"And," she continued to her friend, "when Joseph died of COVID I was almost glad. He nearly disinherited me as well, his own wife, for voting for Hillary Clinton in 2016!"

"No! He voted for Trump?"

"My husband did. He loved Trump's apparent racism and bigotry against blacks and brown people, and Trump's son-in-law is Jewish, so Joseph thought Trump was a good candidate, after all, loyal to Jews."

"But he disinherited your son only for marrying a staunch Catholic?"

"Yes. And it's a shame she's kept her grandfather's uniform, probably thinking he couldn't have been that bad, after all... But here's the incredible end to it all. Believe it or not, Ellen just won the state lottery with a lottery ticket, three million dollars, last week, and she and Jacob are going to Bermuda for a holiday and buying a new house in the Hamptons, so that's their revenge on my husband!" Mrs. Weinberg smiled. "Can you believe it? I'm so happy for them, being together and finding peace after the reading of my husband's selfish will, I'm moving in with them at the new house into the in-laws apartment, and I'll be set for life! And Ellen really isn't so bad. She just got a job working at a synagogue as their Finance CEO, so how anti-Semitic could she be, anyway? She's really quite nice."

Mrs. Weinberg's friend smiled.

"She's probably just rather misled about World War II. And just think! The lottery saved her and your son! And you won't have to take care of your husband Joseph anymore—I know he ran you off your feet!"

"He did."

With that, the two women finished at the cash register, walked away, and I was free to pay for my stockings. I worried a little that I'd be late back to the office, but I'd already gotten an answer to my questions about the disinheritance, and a story about Nazis and marital cheating and murder and the lottery! I paid for my merchandise and walked back to work.

And just this afternoon I had to type another will, this time about a father leaving his ten million dollar fortune to his single daughter, because she was voting for Biden—he apparently loves Biden, and loves his daughter for supporting him, because Biden is a Democrat and this old man has never trucked with Republicans. He's a Liberal and, amazingly, many years ago was tried for murder, also. But he was exonerated, too, because the victim was the lover of his own wife, and actually committed suicide and made it look like murder to get revenge. He took a dose of poison and made it look as though this man had done it, even writing a death note about having been poisoned by the old man.

Unbelievable. There's no end to the stories I hear at this law firm. So tonight I'm going home to play Backgammon with my lover, and we'll toast to each other with vodka-and-tonics that our simple lives are far less complicated than the lives of oh-so-careful, religious millionaires. And we are both Protestant and have no issues about how our children will be raised, and we don't ever expect to make a lot of money. But my life is good, even though I'm middle class and don't have a lot. I have my lover, who just last night told me he got a raise at his job as an accountant and has never voted for the right wing, and never expects to.

Still I wonder why last night he was so insistent on our writing our wills, and to seeing mine once I'd finished writing it? I'm only 32, and it's true he had an affair with a very rich socialite just a year ago. They met at an event we attended for a charity at the Plaza Hotel. The two of them were hot-and-heavy for six months, and I was enormously disturbed and jealous and insecure, but I stayed in our frayed relationship because I love him so much. He's a dedicated Democrat and loves my cooking. But he makes me nervous because he has a temper. Once he shoved me against the kitchen door for serving dinner late. And he bought a gun last week—he said it was to protect us from intruders. His affair with the socialite finally ended...I'm not entirely sure why...maybe it's because he discovered she was leaving him nothing in her will.

###

A CONSTANT MAN

Johnny, at age 47, thought he recalled how it all happened, but tonight he felt like a character out of the Rashomon story, remembering things vaguely and wondering if he was developing dementia or Alzheimer's too. Drinking whisky alone, for he was unmarried and childless, he sat in his living room in sorrow and grief.

***

In the beginning, there was a car with two passengers. Johnny was seven years old. His mother was in her 30s.

"Where are we going, Mommy?"

"I don't know."

"But where are we going?" He paused. "Why did you wake me up to get in the car?"

"Your father has a new girlfriend."

"Since when?"

"I don't know. Since last night. Stop asking questions."

"But who is she?"

"I don't know. Stephanie something-or-other."

"Will I like her?"

"I hope not."

"Do you like her?"

"Who are you kidding? I haven't even met her."

"But do you think you'd like her if you met her?"

The mother paused.

"That's a really dumb question, kid. You're smart. You figure it out."

"Well, are we ever going back home?"

"That remains to be seen."

"But where are we going now?"

"I said, stop asking questions. I don't know. The country, maybe. Maybe we'll stay at an inn. Maybe we'll drive all day, up to Maine, to your grandparents."

"That would be fun. Mommy?"

"Yes?"

"Will I ever see Daddy again?"

"That's the million-dollar question."

"Because I love Daddy."

"All right. That's it. We're turning around and going home."

"What for? What about Grandma and Grandpa's?"

The mother turned the car around and they headed home.

***

Ten years later, the mother and Johnny were on a train. Johnny was now seventeen. The mother spoke first.

"God, I wish it would stop raining. I can hardly see a thing out this window. Are you looking forward to seeing the campus? You know, you might be spending the next four years at this place."

"Yes."

"You don't sound too excited."

"Well, I haven't seen it yet."

"Yes, but it's a good school and it would make your father and I very proud if you went there." She paused. "You can do anything, you know. You could be an architect, an astronaut. There's nothing you can't do."

"I know. Mom?"

"What?"

"Remember the trip we took when I was seven and you ran away from Dad?"

"I didn't run away. We went back, remember?"

"And you never got divorced. Why not?"

"Because I realized I was better off with him than without him."

Suddenly there was a loud crash and they both jerked in their seats. The mother screamed.

"Jesus Christ! Did we hit something?"

"I don't know," said Johnny. "Could've been a cow. We're in the country. There are cows in the fields."

The mother grimaced.

"Great. Now the lights are out. Complete darkness."

"We didn't get hurt. Mom, you're too pessimistic. We'll get there eventually."

"What are you talking about? This is a major inconvenience."

"Want me to get you a cheese sandwich?" Johnny tried to be assuaging.

"The club car's probably closed."

"Mom, I'm glad you didn't leave Dad."

"Well, I could have, you know."

'"He used to play catch with me in the backyard."

"He's paying your tuition for college."

"When we drove back home that day he had tears in his eyes when we walked in the door."

"Good. I didn't notice."

"Well, I did. And he never cheated on you again. It was a one-time thing."

"Well, maybe it was."

"But you never had any more kids."

"One was enough."

"Because it's too much trouble?"

"No, because it's too expensive. Just remember. You can do anything you want, Johnny."

They sat together for a while until whatever damage had been done to the train was repaired, then they were on their way again.

***

It was 20 years later. Johnny was 37, his mother was 60. They were in a room in her home. This time Johnny spoke first.

"When you called I was worried. Are you sick?"

"No."

"Then what was it? You said it was urgent that I come over."

"When your father died I had no idea what his assets were. I thought he'd leave me something."

"He didn't?"

"He left nothing. He was nearly bankrupt. Spent it all."

"I'll help you, Mom. I have a good job."

"I know. Thank God for that PhD. But that's not the worst of it. It's what he spent the money on. I found the receipts. He kept an apartment in the next town for years for that woman of his. All those years. I had no idea."

"Mom, you're imagining things. He never saw her again."

"I found the proof."

"Mom, are you taking your medication?"

"None of your business."

"It's important. Your doctor said so. And he doesn't want you to have alcohol."

"There's nothing wrong with me a little drink can't fix."

"You drink too much. Ever since Dad died. He never cheated on you again, I'm sure of it, after that one time."

"Oh, yes he did. Just wondering. Did you come for dinner?"

"No. Only for a visit."

"Because I didn't cook anything."

"I didn't expect you to."

"Hm. You were a brilliant child, Johnny. All your teachers said so."

"Thanks, Ma."

"You could have done anything. You ended up a professor."

"I like teaching."

"But you don't believe me that your father kept seeing that woman. Then what were those receipts for?"

"Ma, they're probably the rental for his real estate office. He paid a high rent. And you know the company went through a bad spell for a while. You imagine a lot of things, you know that?"

"Maybe. Do you want dinner?"

"You didn't cook anything."

"I thought I peeled some potatoes. Or was that yesterday?"

"I'm leaving now, Ma." Johnny got up from his chair.

"I should have put a roast in the oven."

"I'm not here to eat, Ma. Next time." He leaned over and kissed her cheek, then went home, depressed.

***

It was five years later. Johnny was 42. They were together again, at a nursing home. In front of his mother was a tray with a half-eaten sandwich on it and a plastic cup of milk.

"Are they taking good care of you here?"

"It's all right."

"I want you to be comfortable."

"You should have brought me flowers."

"Sometimes I do."

"You should have brought your wife, too."

"Hm?" Johnny's mind was wandering off.

"Your wife."

"I don't have a wife, Ma."

"You do."

"No."

"Why do you lie to me? I went to your wedding. Didn't I?"

"All right, I had a wife."

"Wasn't she lovely?"

"Who?"

"Your wife."

"Oh. Yes. Yes, I guess she was."

"But she cheated on you."

"What?"

"Just like my husband. …Johnny."

"Huh?"

"What was the name of that woman who lived next to us? A long time ago. I can't remember her name."

"I don't either."

"The one who wore short skirts."

"There wasn't any woman like that."

"Sonya. Or Susan. Or Sadie, or something."

"Next door?"

"They were neighbors. Her husband had an affair, too."

"Ma—"

"I knew it. I just knew. He always came home late."

"I don't know who you're talking about. The man next door was in sales. He traveled."

The mother laughed derisively.

"A traveling salesman? That's how he got away with it."

"With what?"

"The cheating."

"Aw, Jesus, Ma—"

"What was her name? His wife."

"I don't think he had one."

"And what was the name of the man who lived down the street who took care of our washing machine?"

"The plumber? I don't remember. Patrick, or Perkins, or something. Jesus, Ma, you keep asking the same questions over and over again. I don't remember the guy's name. Or Sadie's name."

"Our neighbor was Sadie?"

"I don't know. You said that might have been her name."

"I think it was Susan."

"I have no clue." Johnny felt impatient.

"I'm hungry."

"You just had lunch."

"I didn't touch it."

"I'll tell one of the nurses."

"Tell Ruth. She's nice. She combs my hair."

"I'll tell Ruth."

"I like the pineapple upside-down cake here."

"I'll let them know."

"Didn't you tell me something about Safeway burning down?"

"Yes. Last month."

"I thought it was only a few days ago."

"No. I'm not sure, it happened a month or so ago."

"Someone set it on fire?"

"No. I told you. It was an electrical fire. You forgot."

"All this time I thought it was teenagers." The mother knocked over her plastic cup of milk.

"Ma—you spilled your milk."

"Johnny. Did the store burn to the ground?"

With a sigh, Johnny took a napkin from her tray and mopped up the milk on the floor. But he didn't answer.

"I'm glad you came today," said his mother. "Thank you for the flowers."

"I didn't bring any. Next time I will."

"It's been months since I've seen you."

"It's been a week." Johnny paused. "Forget it."

"You don't come often enough. Thank you for the flowers, anyway."

Johnny leaned over and kissed her on the cheek.

"Bye, Ma." He left and felt despair.

***

It was two months later. Johnny was in his car talking on a cell phone.

"When you say it's non-specific, does that mean reversible? ...Oh. They're two different things? ...Because it seems reversible to me. ...Only ten percent are? ...Well, you're a doctor, you'd know. ...I just thought, since she fell down a flight of stairs when she was 63, maybe it was reversible. I mean, I thought maybe the fall caused a brain injury, but that at some point she could recover. ...Uh-huh. ...Well, it's very frustrating. She doesn't know what month it is or even what year it is sometimes. I'm beginning to wonder if she knows who I am. ...Well, could she ever be a danger to herself? ...Probably not. That's good. But she does get angry suddenly. ...It's called a catastrophic reaction? ... Listen, listen to me—she was always kind of that way anyway. No need to make more out of it than it is. ...Uh-huh. ...Uh-huh. ...Look, can you just make sure she's comfortable? I want her to have food she likes and some company, someone to talk to. …She's got a lot of anxiety about my father. …No, he's dead. She thinks he was always unfaithful. …"Paranoia can develop in some patients." Well, she believed it most of her married life. She was on risperidone for years. …Look, I'll probably meet you next week. We can talk then. …Thanks. Appreciate it."

He disconnected his phone.

***

It was five years later. Johnny was now 47. He was in a hearse on his way to his mother's funeral, in tears, and had a letter in his hand. He was talking to himself.

"Ma, you were the greatest. Always talking me up to myself, telling me I could do anything. Even in this letter. But you lost your mind. When did it start? With Dad? He never fooled around after that one time. I don't think he did. You lost your mind. When did it begin? The earliest seeds of it? In your thirties? Your forties? I'll never know. The doctors said it was early onset. And the whole thing with Dad. The affair you thought he kept having… He never did. I'm sure of it. You were distrustful. You always made a big deal out of everything."

Johnny paused.

"It wasn't his fault. Even if he did cheat. Not altogether. You lacked forgiveness, Ma. You always carried some kind of bitterness around with you… Weren't you proud when I graduated from college? At least I can be happy for that. I'm sorry I never made you a grandmother."

Johnny began biting his nails and kept talking to himself.

"The meds. Delusional without them, your doctor said. And those nursing home visits! Jesus! You kept asking the same questions, over and over again. How much can a person take? You know what I think, Ma? You were a very fragile woman. All your life. Very insecure. Yes, that's it. You were fragile."

With a tremor in his voice, Johnny read from his mother's letter and could hear her ghostly voice speaking out loud to him. The voice made him feel like a corpse himself.

"You were wrong about me, Johnny," he thought he heard his mother's voice say. "Smart, but lacking perception. I was strong. I coped. I forgave your father's affair, until I found out it had gone on longer than I'd thought. And what a grown child thinks about these things is a mystery to me. How you still loved your father, after I told you, and after he died. You still wanted me to love his memory. But I couldn't. And the main thing is, I always did love you.

Remember that. It takes a lot to stay with an inconstant man. So remember that some day if you suffer the indignity of staying with someone you no longer love. It's like looking out of the window of a train in a downpour. You're going somewhere, but there's no light in sight, and no end in view to the darkness, just the steady thudding of the rain against the window, like hearing your heartbeat at night when you wonder if he's ever coming home. An inconstant man. That was your father, Johnny. I hope you'll forgive me for telling you."

Johnny crumpled up the letter in his hand, then wiped his eyes and let out a sob. He felt as if he were in the Rashomon tale, not knowing what the truth was, not knowing what to believe. He cried out to his mother's memory.

"*I* was a constant man, Ma! *I* was!"

Then he drove home to his empty house to drink alone.

###

THE WATER FAIRY & THE LEGEND OF SHAVONNE

Once there was a country town filled with farming people and which had a neighboring kingdom, but there was one blight upon the land—a dangerous witch.

The Killigarne witch, so evil—she'd turned green from envy, her skin, and even her dresses were tinged green—resented fair Shavonne, who had pale skin and hair as dark as pitch. Shavonne was born in Killigarne, known for its beautiful women, and she did a bit of farming herself.

But the witch, jealous of Shavonne's lovely face, turned even greener upon seeing Shavonne's slippers. Shavonne had been given these on her 18th birthday by a fairy who appeared before her in her bedroom.

Her bedroom, poor and unfurnished, had only in it a four-poster bed and a stand with a pitch and a washing basin filled with water. One night when Shavonne was washing up and getting ready for bed, she lit a candle and poured some water into the basin. To her alarm, a fairy escaped from the top of the pitcher, a fairy with pink wings and pink cheeks, and it flew around the room.

"Don't be afraid," the fairy said. "I've come with a gift, to make your life better and more magical, and I bring no danger with me."

With that, the fairy laid a little pair of slippers at Shavonne's feet, and just as quickly disappeared back into the pitcher.

Shavonne was dumbstruck. She'd never seen a water fairy before—or, indeed, any fairies at all! Carefully, she donned the slippers and shivered a little, but soon felt their cozy warmth and furry comfort.

"Will these magic slippers protect me from now on?" she asked no one in particular, since the fairy had disappeared. But she heard the fairy's faint and gentle voice wafting out of the water pitcher.

"Of course! You'll always be protected. And just so you know, the evil witch who causes so much destruction in these parts tried to cut my wings off once, but I escaped. I was trying to do good, and she resented me." And then the fairy's light voice was silenced, and Shavonne heard from her no more that night.

She shuddered—how could a witch try to clip a fairy's wings? She'd never until now been much of a believer in an enchanted world, but now she was convinced such mystery existed. She paced back and forth on her wooden floor, dwelling on magic and surprises and feeling endlessly grateful to the fairy.

She examined her slippers. Made of rabbit's fur they were, and brown like little otters basking in the sandy stream where Shavonne went swimming every day. Her feet were warm and coddled in the slippers, but finally she took them off to go to sleep, and placed them careful at the foot of her bed.

She woke early the next morning and again marvelled at the fairy who had been so kind the night before. Then she removed her nightgown and donned her clothes for the day. Shavonne dressed carefully, and simply, like a peasant—but she had personal charms and dainty, cupcake-like breasts, and shapely legs, and her hair, her most prized trait, hung long and thick to her waist. She hoped one day to enchant an upright man, someone kind and loyal, who'd partner her through life and with whom she'd have many children.

So the witch, who had a turreted castle on a hill nearby, did her best to punish Shavonne. She saw Shavonne wearing her new fur slippers one morning in the garden, and, on her bicycle, tried to knock Shavonne over.

"You wicked thing," cried Shavonne. "You'll get justice! And now I have these magic slippers to protect me!"

Over the next month the witch, in her turreted castle, tried potions and spells to cast Shavonne out of her wicked kingdom that she ruled with an iron fist, but Shavonne was strong and found new power in the authority the fairy's gift of slippers had given her.

One day she went walking in the woods, not especially afraid of encountering the witch on her bicycle, for she knew now she was protected. By chance she met a handsome prince from the neighboring country who was hunting a fox. Shavonne asked him why he'd strayed so far from his own part of the country, and he answered with a smile.

"I heard there was a lovely maiden hereabouts, and wanted to meet her. She's pale with long, black hair, I'm told, and as kind as anything one would hope to encounter in the forest or the meadows or on the road. And I have met her!"

Shavonne smiled back—he was flattering her! But in the nicest way, and she knew he was genuine in his praise, for he got off his steed and knelt before her. Then, taken by her beauty, he offered her his carriage that had followed him for the capture of the fox, and offered her a ride home.

Amazed by his majestic generosity, Shavonne accepted the ride. She'd not only never until recently met a fairy, but she'd also never met a prince! For Shavonne had no dowry and no prospects; she'd been poor and shabby all her wasted, sorry life—and, when she met the prince while walking in the woods, she knew the fairy's good wishes for her had come true!

Once home, Shavonne sat by the fire and prayed for the return of the prince, for he had told her he'd take her on a picnic the following week, and

Shavonne was already planning what treats she'd bake for him for that special day.

But the witch persisted in her evil ways—Shavonne found out from a peasant neighbor three days later that the witch had paid a visit to the prince, and offered to him her own daughter, Grisella, not a beauty but a virgin anyhow, a fact the witch boasted of. The witch, you see, was thinking that no other girl could be that attractive to the prince, who, if the truth be known, must have a virgin bride.

Shavonne had once been betrothed to a local boy, a farmer, who'd drowned in the river. And the prince had recently heard of this and wondered if Shavonne was pure. But all the witch's potions and spells did not deter the prince, for he knew Grisella was a selfish, cruel wretch and he intended to ask Shavonne herself if she'd never had a lover. Surely this beautiful girl couldn't lie!

One day before their picnic, Shavonne met Grisella near a stream while tending to the goats, and Grisella spat upon Shavonne and stole her furry slippers.

"I'll fix you," Grisella said, "My mother's got your number, and we'll see you cast aside by the prince."

Now barefooted, Shavonne wandered through the fields in wonder at Grisella's nasty temper and hoped her prince would come—then, suddenly, along the grassy path George came riding on his steed to rescue her, because his maidservant, gathering bluebells for a bouquet for the dinner table, had seen it all.

"I have to ask you," said the prince apologetically. "I knew you had a friend who drowned, but didn't know how close you were. It's stipulated in my father's will that I must marry a virgin."

"Good saints alive!" said Shavonne in return. "I've never given my virginity to any man, and never would without the sanctity of marriage, and I'm as pure as woodland snow, that same white snow that falls on treetops and over all the fields and your castle, too!"

Impressed and believing her, the prince offered her a kiss, which she gladly accepted. The prince then opened a satchel hanging from his saddle, and gave her shoes made of Spanish leather to replace her stolen slippers, and when Shavonne donned them she felt a little shiver of love.

It was nearing nightfall and the witch, upon her bicycle while riding through the fields, had spied them and called out praying they'd go to Hell. But Shavonne was merry anyway, knowing she was safe, and told the prince she loved him, and when he asked for her hand in marriage she immediately consented.

Just then the pink-cheeked, pink-winged fairy Shavonne had thought she'd never see again flew up from the stream she and the prince stood near— the water fairy again! The weather abruptly changed, there was sudden rain, and owing to the fairy the witch was frozen by hailstones that fell like rocks upon her but didn't touch the prince or Shavonne.

"My gift of good fortune to you was permanent," whispered the fairy, "And not even Grisella can take it away." Then just as quickly as she'd appeared, the fairy vanished back into the stream and Shavonne wondered if the prince had even seen or heard her. No matter—she had, and her joyful future was cast. The prince gave her a ride home through the romantic rain on the back of his steed. Grisella, seeking out her mother that night, died a sorry death after catching fever in the tempest, so Shavonne had no rival anymore.

The prince married Shavonne two months later, for Shavonne was kind and good and had won him in the end, like all good beauties will when faced with jealousy and spite and wrongful acts. They lived together in their home, a palace like no other, built of chalky fieldstones, with chimneys by the score.

And when they did have children, their babes were just as lovely as one might have guessed from gazing at their parents. Shavonne nicknamed the youngest "Pinky," after her not-forgotten fairy friend, who had been her angel of mercy.

Years later when the prince and Shavonne got old, they never had regrets at seeing the old witch and her unappealing offspring die such lonely deaths, for truth and sacrifice win out, and justice will be done to peasant girls who wait and hope for love that's glittering and fine, eternal like the sun.

###

FAVOR

Stephen, age seven, and discouraged by his strict teacher, Mrs. Bancroft, wondered if he'd ever get an "A"—or even a "B"—on his report card. All he ever got were "C"s.

One day at school when the children were learning about plants, Stephen said he loved fall 'foilage'. Surely using such a big word in second grade would earn Mrs. Bancroft's respect.

But she looked stern, saying, "The correct word is 'foliage', Stephen. You said *'foilage.'*"

Stephen blushed with embarrassment and made up his mind to keep his mouth shut the rest of the day. How could he have gotten the word wrong? He thought he'd read it in a fairy tale.

But Mrs. Bancroft went on with the class.

"Now, children, this is important. *Never cheat.* Not on tests, not at home. It'll prevent you from earning respect, getting into college, and even becoming President of the United States!"

Stephen stifled a laugh—as if he'd ever run for President, poor student that he was.

A week later, Mrs. Bancroft handed out report cards for the year's end. She looked tired, probably from staying up the night before marking them, and as Steven took the envelope provided for his parents, he shuddered thinking what bad marks he'd get again.

He trudged home and handed the envelope to his mother when he arrived. She grimaced while tearing it open—she didn't expect good results. But to Stephen's surprise, she was soon beaming.

"You got all "A"s!" she exclaimed, and wrapped him in her arms. "Well done!"

Stephen couldn't believe it until she handed the card to him. Sure enough, under Math, Social Studies, Spelling, even Attitude & Development, he had scored all "A"s! He asked his mother if they could have something special for dinner to celebrate.

"We'll have mac & cheese, just like every Friday night—but I'll make a chocolate cake just for you!"

Stephen grinned and thought about how proud he'd be when his father got home and when he got back to school on Monday.

But on Monday, he walked into the classroom and Mrs. Bancroft gave him her usual disapproving look.

"Why are you frowning?" asked Stephen in disappointment. "You gave me all "A"s last week."

"I certainly did not," answered Mrs. Bancroft sourly. Then she picked up her copies of all the report cards and leafed through to find his.

"Good grief!" she exclaimed. "What have I done?"

Stephen held his breath.

"I'm sorry," said Mrs. Bancroft. "I was very tired Thursday night and I copied exactly the marks I'd made on Allison Patrick's report card. Hers came right in front of yours. I apologize. But there's nothing I can do about it now. I've already handed in the results to the Principal."

Stephen was grief-stricken. He had to say something.

"But—you cheated! And you just told us last week never to cheat. You shouldn't have copied the grades you gave on Allison's card!"

Mrs. Bancroft sighed and looked very displeased with herself.

"Stephen, I have to admire you. You hold people to account. Do you know what that means?"

"It means I expect them to tell the truth. And you just did."

Mrs. Bancroft offered a smile, a rare one for her, and plucked the rose out of the vase on her desk.

"I'm giving you this rose because I want to make it up to you. Take it home to your mother—she'll like it." And with that, Mrs. Bancroft stood and crossed to the blackboard to begin the first lesson of the day. Stephen went to sit at his usual desk holding the prickly rose.

That afternoon he returned home, deciding not to tell his mother the bad news. What harm could there be in a report card full of "A"s, even if it had been a mistake? He handed her the rose, told her it was from Mrs. Bancroft, and his mother looked thrilled.

"Thanks, my smart, precious boy!"

He wasn't sorry. She was happy.

And the truculent Mrs. Bancroft wasn't sorry either, to tell the truth. She knew she'd always had it in for Stephen, but he was a gentle kid with respect for others, and he'd confronted her fairly, and she resolved from now on to treat him better. She'd never meant to be cruel.

And, as the music teacher Mr. Sullivan was always chanting in the hallway, "Every Good Boy Deserves Favor."

###

THE STATUE OF THE LEAPING HARE,
A Story of Magic

(After sculptor Barry Flanagan's "Leaping Hare & Crescent Bell," 1988)

A little boy, age five, was standing in a gallery in London. It was his birthday. His mother had carelessly wandered off, leaving him to his own childlike devices. The little boy, whose name was Andrew, stood in front of a statue. It looked like something out of a picture book. Suddenly the statue turned its head towards him—or did it really? Too young to recognize the fever of a wild imagination, the little boy moved closer.

"Yes, come near where you can hear me," whispered the statue. "I speak low for fear of adults, who'd never understand."

Andrew nodded and leaned in to hear the statue better.

"You're probably wondering who I am and how I got here," said the statue. "I'm a hare. You've heard of creatures like me, but probably never before seen a statue of one. I was built by an artist, in tribute to my own kind, and to children."

Andrew smiled at that—after all, *he* was a child and no statue had ever spoken to him before. The hare seemed to be talking in what Andrew believed to be poetry—soft, lilting words with lots of pauses and room to take a breath. His kindergarten teacher had read children's poetry to his class a few times, so he knew what poetry was. The statue spoke again.

"Bark and twigs? Yes, I eat bark and twigs—
At least my brethren do.
A hare! Not "rabbit"—I repeat, a hare.
Do you know the difference?"

"I do now," answered Andrew carefully.

"Rabbits, loathsome creatures,
Have short ears and no black markings
And they don't turn white in winter!
Imagine that!"

Andrew smiled again. His uncle had a farm in the north and he'd heard Uncle Richard complain about the problem of rabbits eating his carefully-planted vegetables.

"And as a statue, in this spot, I've found a niche," the hare continued.
"After all, how many bronze hares
Grace London galleries?
I'm quite a masterpiece
And quite a piece of magic!"

"*I* think you are, too," said Andrew with respect. The hare, undeterred by nearby adults, continued speaking his poetry.

"As for the oft-asked question—
Why leap over the moon? As I do now.
Because I'm happy. What more can I say?
And the bell you see here? I like chimes."

"What's a chime?" asked Andrew. He was cautious to speak quietly in case one of the adults closing in heard him and told him not to talk to statues. He knew how pompous adults could be, with little understanding of people as young as he. The hare answered his question.

"A chime gives off a ringing tone!
And by the by, who'd want to eat a hare?
I wasn't meant for that—
Too precious for such nonsense,

And full of sorcery.
Magicians have been known
To pull us out of hats—
Along with rabbits, too!"

That made Andrew laugh. He'd seen a magician pull a rabbit out of a hat at a holiday party for a friend. But how could a person eat a metal statue? He knew what the hare meant, though—the statue was just talking about his kindred animals.

As if he could read Andrew's thoughts, the hare continued…
"Yet, still a pest to some,
The farmers hate me.
I represent a threat to all their crops.
But hares have mystery, as do statues."

The hare raised his voice a little in indignation and Andrew looked around to make sure no one else could overhear and tell him not to talk to strangers.

"Am I just a roguish thing?"
"I'm no threat—
I'm agile and I jump
And entertain the children."

"I like you even if others think you're a beast," said Andrew. The hare spoke again.

"Yes—think of me as graceful
And fantastic, when next time
You see me with this crescent moon!
And, of course, Happy Birthday, kind one!"

"How did you know it was my birthday?" asked Andrew, puzzled at this unusual creature.

"I can read minds. That's something few realize about statues. We've got little else to do when we're so stationary. Your mother, off in the distance, is watching you and will be back soon. She sees from a distance that you're fascinated by me. And when you have your birthday cake tonight after dinner, I hope you'll blow out your five candles in one breath, and wish for me a long and happy life here in London. I hope I haven't bored you."

"No!" exclaimed Andrew. "I love what you've told me. And I will wish for you a long and happy life."

"The same to you. You deserve one, little boy. And now go meet your mother."

Andrew saw his Mum approaching and ran up to her.

"I just had a chat with a statue," he told her.

"Nonsense," she said, but smiled. "But I'm glad you found a friend."

Andrew shrugged off her disbelief, and together they walked out and down along the street where red buses passed and the black cabs of London were whizzing by. Andrew, little as he was, felt as if he'd been let in on a secret, and knew he'd had a taste of an artist's magic.

###

NO WAY I'M GOING TO REUNION

My 50th high school reunion is to be held at the Marriott—that hotel for medium-priced rooms and, well, high school reunions. And the organizers sent me a nice, engraved invitation, and my old friend Gena, from twelfth grade, messaged me on Facebook asking if I was going to go.

But I don't want to go. Not for any good reason, really—I just don't want to expose my aging self to all those nobodies who ignored me in high school.

I ignored a few people myself. There was Kathy Sales, who's probably still unmarried—I've been married three times, for God's sake!—and she was a nerd like no other. Could hardly walk and chew gum at the same time, to quote that old cliche. I actually asked her to be my Vice President when I was elected to office senior year. Yes! I was elected President of my class!

Does it sound like I was popular? I wasn't. I was just committed to ending the Vietnam war; that's why kids voted for me. I was radical and dedicated to "The Cause," and Kathy was very awkward and I felt sorry for her—but believe me, that doesn't mean I want to see her again today. And even though I got elected President of my class, and gave the speech on graduation day, I still felt like such a loser. Because I was flat-chested then and awful at sports and had never been kissed. The terror of being a teenager!

And then there was Mike, the editor of the school paper. Always thought he was smarter than everyone else and ended up attending Harvard, for college. He dated a friend of mine, who also went into journalism. But he told me once I wasn't a real woman because I didn't have boobs. The callous type. Why would I want to see him again?

Then there was Rudolph, who was heavily into rock & roll music. But unlike him, I wasn't that "cool." My idea of "hip" was the Carpenters—Richard and the famous Karen, who ended up dying of anorexia nervosa, something, thank God, I've never suffered from myself. In fact, I have the opposite problem—I gain weight easily. Sometimes it's misery. Anyway, Rudolph was into the band Genesis. Their drummer, Phil Collins, wound up being a huge star in the '80s, singing and writing on his own. I think he had a bunch of Number One songs. But I wasn't to discover that interesting fact until much later. Rudolph was too sophisticated for me, with his taste in music and the motorcycle he rode around between classes, on the paved strip between our high school's two buildings.

I hated high school. I felt like a loner, wandering through the hallways with my books tucked under my arm, not being cool, and being so vehemently opposed to Vietnam. Today, when I look back, it seems prescient—after all, kids now are all excited about climate change, so maybe they and my old self at the age of 16 aren't so different. I admire kids today. They don't seem racist or sexist, generally speaking, and they have open minds. But not everyone was like that when I was in high school.

And another reason I don't want to go to my reunion is the food. A whole lot of clam dip and pigs-in-blankets—that's what in my day we called wieners that were wrapped up in some kind of biscuit stuff. The thing is, I'm a vegetarian and I hate that crap. I haven't eaten meat in 20 years. My kids turned me against it and I never looked back. So why would I go to my high school reunion, even just for the food?

Do I sound like a snob? I probably am—after all, what could go wrong at a high school reunion? Just blabbing with a lot of people you knew decades ago—"You haven't changed a bit! How do you do it?" "I love your hairstyle! What salon do you go to?" "I'm in finance. Where do you work?" All the typical questions one would ask of someone one hasn't seen in years—and don't miss at all.

My oldest, Tiffany, says, "Mom, just go for the fun of it! You'll see forgotten friends and probably have a good time!" Well, she would if she went to her own high school reunion. She's a social butterfly, totally unlike me at that age. I sometimes wonder if she really is my own child—but I gave birth to her, so she must be.

"The fun of it." I don't think so. The prospect of seeing all those sorry kids again now that they've grown up seems dismal to me. Anyway, my husband's having an affair with his secretary and that's kind of preoccupying me right now. I keep wondering if he'll divorce me, or if I'll divorce him first. We're having a battle about it. There's a lot of money at stake—we're both bankers.

So those are all the reasons why I don't feel like going to my high school reunion. ...Jesus! I just took a look at my graduation photo, in my old yearbook, and do I look like a jerk in the picture! Fake gold necklace, sleeveless black nylon T-shirt, with a cheesy smile on my face. I looked something like the shy sister of Alfred E. Neuman on the cover of MAD Magazine. Stupid grin, missing a front tooth, but that was before I got a bridge for my teeth. Do I really want to remember that terrible age?

Nope. Not going to my reunion. Now, my college reunion, that's another story. In college I was a success and found my niche. I'd grown up a little, had my first lover, was a star at academics, and loved my roommate. I'd go to that reunion in a heartbeat. But high school? No way. Fug-ged-about-it!!

And then when it's over, I'll have to read a report on all the goings-on from my old friend Gena, messaging me on Facebook. Excruciating—hearing about who looked good, who's aged terribly, and who's already died. No thanks. Gena can keep those observations to herself. I really, really, don't even want to know. I must sound like a crank. But that's how I honestly feel. And that's the end of that.

###

THE PUNISHING FACE OF DEBT

Sometimes the only thought I wake up with is paying off debt. It's like the Heavens above shaking a finger at me on an hourly basis. It's like God himself exacting punishment. It involves my identity as a supposedly responsible, self-supporting American—the kind of which Trump himself would approve—as if I care what he thinks.

I have two degrees and I'm a writer. I get miniscule payments here and there. Almost enough to buy a new tube of mascara. I cheerfully submit my work all the time to fly-by-night and even respectable journals and contests. But I do other work for real money, just to stuff my hungry face...cashiering, ushering at theatres, giving long winded, gassy tours at historic landmarks and museums...

Then a friend kindly said, when I got hired part-time at a law office—and it's hardly as if I liked the job—don't give up your position. It's salvation! Pay off your crummy debt. Don't you want to be self-sufficient?—your parents didn't shell out money for college so you could end up in the poorhouse. She made me feel like a basketcase. But her advice was solid. After all, how many manicures do I want to suffer through after chewing my nails over how much I owe my creditors? She knew what she was talking about. But wouldn't you just know, I got laid off at the law firm. And now, applying for full-time positions where I'm interviewed by condescending, 30-year-old naifs, I can tell when I walk in they're thinking, "Great, Grandma's here and we can sit back and chuckle." I'm left thinking, am I really a geezer? My identity as a striving, resilient resident of wonderful, thrifty New England is at stake.

My old boss despised me for sitting down as a cashier at a clothing store; he wanted me to stand for a whole shift. When I usher for theatres that are paying me less per hour than the cost of a ticket, I unwillingly stand on my feet for hours, too. And as a tour guide I got fed up listening to the drone of my own voice. I sounded bored as hell describing the virtues and beauty of Tiffany stained glass windows—which were, indeed, lovely, but the fact that the job was in a historic church only made me feel the good Lord was wagging his finger at me yet again. I had to consider my self-hood—was I going to be a babbling automaton with an aching back for the rest of my life?

So I decided, with renewed enthusiasm, to attempt raising money for a political party. Consider this: I always vote Democratic. My parents did. My grandparents did. They believed in government and helping those worse off, the kind of people I unrealistically hope I don't become. I'd be doing something admirable by fundraising for Democrats. A big attraction was that I could sit at a desk—I'd developed nasty rheumatoid arthritis that made me feel 20 years older than I was.

It wasn't going to make me rich. Paying only minimum wage, plus $2.00 per credit card donation I earned, it was at best a good cause and would generate enough income to buy new lipstick—maybe in a shade called Political Pink. But could I actually make the minimum number of donations? And would I succeed at convincing people to part with a hundred dollars a shot? The optimistic Hiring Recruiter thought so—he said I could start in three days. My identity miraculously recovered, like Trump after contracting COVID, and I had a new job!

Arriving my first night, a small group of us sat in a classroom and were taught the risky ropes of the job—mainly getting rejected a lot on the phone. The second night was the dreary same thing—I thought I'd collapse out of boredom—and on the third day of training there was a test of our burgeoning knowledge of Congress and the Senate. I felt like I was in a Civics class in high school all over again. On the fourth day we would—praise be!—be let go live on the phone. We'd stick to carefully-worded and rigidly defined scripts on our monitors and were expected to get one credit card donation an hour, which seemed vaguely do-able, if I could stand being turned down a lot by irate people answering the phone.

Our trainer was a man missing his two front teeth and wearing the same outfit, a scruffy hoodie and a down vest, every night, but he was impressively knowledgeable about American politics. Sarcastic about Republicans, he said they were poorly-informed idiots and that he'd always done this type of work. I liked him the same way I liked Bernie Sanders—he was a little crazy. Amazingly, I scored 100% correct on my test after a week's training, which puffed me up like a feathered bird in the winter, and prepared to start work for real the following Monday. I felt affirmed in my knowledge of government and thought, "Gee—maybe this is something I'll actually excel at, and I'll make good on that education my parents wasted so much money on."

The night we went live for an entire shift, we sat in cramped cubicles with headsets and computers, 25 of us. The callers fell into three camps: hungry students, retirees eager for a little income on top of Social Security, and hard-core political types who reminded me of those raggedy protesters I met during the Vietnam war. For legal reasons, no writing implements or cell phones were allowed, because we'd be taking credit card numbers. We also weren't allowed to eat at our desks—chewing while on the phone was considered obnoxious. But I could definitely handle that. I was raised with Emily Post manners.

My female supervisor took me aside the first night and graciously gave me some tips—always profusely thank the person you've called for past support, don't give up until you've given the respondent three earnest pitches, and don't fail to mention that money raised goes to campaigns for the entire Senate and Congress. She wore blue eye shadow carefully dusted onto her half-inch false eyelashes, so obviously she tried to look pretty on the job. I wondered if I should have dressed up a little more than wearing sweatpants. I felt like a slob.

After two luckless hours, I called a man who answered, "Who the f*ck is this?" Only slightly offended, because after all I was rudely interrupting him at dinner, I hung up and dispositioned him to be taken off the call list; no one else should be subjected to obscenity.

Another woman spoke in an artificially "kind" voice when I told her who I was, and said, "Let me interrupt you. I'm going to talk about empowerment. And I'm going to talk about happiness. *But you probably don't even know what those words mean, do you?"* Annoyed because she made me feel like a pesky and pathetic moron, I was told to disposition that as a number to call back—there might be someone else in the household who'd be more receptive later. But I was irritated and felt personally diminished.

Even so, I managed to raise $285.00 that night. I'd already earned my keep—and how good that felt! I was exultant at my "winnings" but worried about talking people out of hard-earned cash. That's the dismaying paradox of fundraising. How much right does one have to mercilessly pepper people at home, asking for money? I knew I was being a pest. A couple of nights later, my arthritis became so painful I turned back on the way to my shift. Not sorry to email the company that I couldn't return, I was relieved.

Look—I don't need jewels I've seen in Town & Country magazine, or a vacation to the

Bahamas—that's not how I identify myself, like a high roller. I just need to stop the insanity of mind-numbing jobs and pay off my damned debt. My lovely friend who advised me has common sense and knows socking money away pays off. She was saying, "Be tough. Be strong. Work like a Turk."

But it's going to be a rough road, like Sisyphus pushing the rock up the mountain. I really should have gone to medical school.

###

THE END

Acknowledgments:

"The Lost Dog" was first published by *Defenestrationism.net* in 2019.

"Such Good Friends" was first published by *Reedsy Prompts*, summer 2020.

"A Conspiracy" was first published by *Defenestrationism.net* in 2019.

"Robbing Peter to Pay Paul" was first published by *Defenestrationism.net* in 2019.

"The Garden of Remembrance" was first published by the *International Human Rights Art Festival Publishes* in 2020.

"A Steady Drip" was first published by *In Case of Emergency Press* in the anthology *One Last Story*, Australia, 2020.

"A Field of Poppies" was first produced as a series of monologues at the Veterans' Festival, Salem State University, Massachusetts, on September 19th, 20th, 21st, 2019, in the Callan Studio Theatre.

"The Affairs of the Rich" was first published by *Reedsy Prompts*, summer 2020.

"No Way I'm Going to Reunion" was first published by *Reedsy Prompts*, fall 2020

...And thank you to Christen Kincaid, my stalwart editor, and to friends Jonathan Kozol, Evan Guilford-Blake, Don Loftus, for their back-cover blurbs, and also to my dear brother James Patterson and sister-in-law Betsy Mangan for always reading my manuscripts when I selfishly ask them to!

Martha Patterson has had plays, essays, poetry, and fiction published in more than 20 literary journals and anthologies (by Applause Books, Pioneer Drama Service, the *Sheepshead Review*, Silver Birch Press, *Syndrome Magazine,* Smith & Kraus, and others), and has had plays produced in 21 states and eight countries. She has two degrees in Theatre from Mount Holyoke College and Emerson College, and lives in Boston, the USA. She loves being surrounded by her books, radio, and laptop.